BROWNSTONE
KIDNAP
CRACKUP

BROWNSTONE KIDNAP CRACKUP

A Max Royster Mystery

by Frank Hickey

PIGTOWN BOOKS

Library of Congress
Catalogue-in-Publication Data

Brownstone Kidnap Crackup / Frank Hickey
1. Fiction – Crime 2. Fiction – Mystery 3. Fiction – Hard-boiled

Published by Pigtown Books

ISBN: 978-0-9848810-3-1

For further information, please contact:

info@pigtownbooks.com

10 9 8 7 6 5 4 3 2 1

First Edition / First Issue

To Miao,

To my family,

To members of Team Larry.
You know who you are.

PROLOGUE

WHUP!

Nancy's palm slugged me.

I staggered back.

By training, my left went out. But she danced away on her toes.

She weaved back. Short muscles bunched all over her body. Her honey-blonde hair waved over baby-blue eyes.

"Five one, one-hundred-and-three pounds," I panted. "And you could kill me with either bare hand."

"Well, Mister Royster," she purred in her Kansas drawl. "I sure wouldn't want to do that. I would miss these sessions."

I tried moving under her guard. She hit me with two strikes against my padded headguard.

"Sometime today," I panted, "the flu will hit me. I can tell. So I have to work out now, two days before Christmas. Or I'll be out of shape for a week."

Her foot tapped my shinguard.

It hurt.

"So you can coast through Christmas using your Department sick leave," she said.

"I'm off The Job, Nancy. They dropped me for what they call 'By Virtue of Mental Disease'."

We were sparring inside her fighting gym in Manhattan's Spanish Harlem. The radio played classic Christmas songs. Notes uncurled through the gym smell of old leather and sneakers.

"That hurts me to hear," she said. "I know how much you adored being a cop who helped losers like me and my man, Santiago. You're still getting checks, right?"

"Not a cent. They want me to fight them for everything, limp home and die of a stress heart attack while frying cheap falafel in my overpriced kitchenette."

"New York's Finest," she said. "Ha!"

"The Irish choirboys running the Job say that they will lock me down in a mental hospital for life if I sue."

"How are you surviving this Christmas season then?" she asked.

"Ducking relatives. In-laws and out-laws. Avoiding fruit-cake desserts."

"Is that all?" she asked.

"Delivering liquor to the elite in the Upper East Side. Where I used to be the Man, patrolling in the blues and giving orders, now I'm hustling for tips from millionaires."

"That is so wrong," she purred. "Anyway, at your age, that's enough workout for today. You know where the showers are."

CB

Stripping off my sweats in the shower room, I could feel the flu take hold in my body.

The hot shower water blessed me.

Then a small hard body gripped me around the hips. Fingernails scratched my flesh. Nancy was nude, showering with me.

"Mister Royster," Nancy whispered. "The front door is locked."

"But everything else is wide open," I said.

"Let me scrub you like a big dog and then lie down with you. You need a private place to recover."

"You have your honeybunch, Santiago, who makes your little heart go pit-a-pat."

"Sure I do. He'll never know."

"But I will. And you remember that I'm in love with somebody else?"

"Who is making you suffer alone," she said.

"Nevertheless," I said.

She ground her body against mine.

Somehow my arm reached up and switched off the water.

— 2 —

Still holding her, I stepped out of the shower and into the big room.

"You look so wretched that I want to cheer you up," she whispered. "Give you something special."

Tchaikovsky's "Nutcracker" music played on the radio. I put us in waltz position.

"I don't feel wretched," I lied. "Watch."

We waltzed naked to the "Nutcracker."

"Tchaikovsky suffered a sad, toxic life," I said. "But hear how happy his music sounds. He and I together can laugh through anything bad."

໒ɔ

Chapter 1

THE EVE OF CHRISTMAS EVE – 4:45 P.M.

Snow was starting to powder Manhattan's Upper East Side where the elite lived. Winter chill edged the air. Nearby, someone was burning Yuletide wood in a fireplace.

I double-parked the van on East 71st Street off Third Avenue. My window was open. The handle was broken. The cold air cut me. As usual, the key stuck in the ignition. I didn't have the three minutes of wrestling it would take to free it. Today was complex enough already.

My winter flu was growing, shaking and headaching me. It sapped whatever strength I had left. So the ignition key stayed. Nobody stole rickety vans like mine in this tony neighborhood, and now I would be just twelve feet away from it.

Last year, I had patrolled the neighborhood, wearing the NYPD uniform.

A case of Château Pontet Canet Pauillac sagged me down more. I hoisted it up to my hip and staggered over to Number 166, a brownstone with Christmas lights winking in the windows.

The door swung outwards.

The impact caught my left elbow. It spun me – six feet and two-twenty pounds – down onto the concrete. The case burst and the wine bottles exploded. My elbow screamed with pain.

"Oh, showers of bastards!" I roared. "There goes my tip!"

Bordeaux and glass splashed my leather bomber jacket, staining the cream sheepskin cuffs purple.

I smelled like a squashed grape.

A man came through the door. He saw me on the ground, kicked and caught my mouth with his heel.

BAM!

A stocking smeared his face, masking it. He gripped a sawed-off shotgun in a gloved hand.

He was robbing the rich, like Robin Hood.

"Get lost, Shotgun," I grunted. "You made your score."

But Shotgun came through the doorway gripping a girl in a red dress. The shotgun barrel had a wire noose taped to it. The noose fitted around her neck. If she moved, the shotgun could blow her head off.

Behind him, women screamed.

Plates smashed on the wall.

A man in a tuxedo tried grabbing Shotgun. But Shotgun elbowed him back onto the vestibule wall without releasing the girl.

The Grabber slid down the wall. Blood stained his gray hair where his head had hit the wall. His plastic eyeglasses slipped off his button nose.

I was suddenly aware of "Silent Night" playing on a stereo upstairs. Cigar smoke flowed out of the doorway and mingled with the swirling snow.

"Watch out for that gun!" another man shouted.

My mouth filled with blood. Shotgun kicked me and connected again. Bones crackled in my neck. I went backwards onto the pool of wine.

My hands gripped his leg. It felt strong and young. He moved like an athlete sideways, breaking my hold.

If he got away, he would rape the girl, then kill her to cover his tracks. Every cop knew that.

I punched at his kidney with all I had. The wallop hit. He gasped and swung the girl around to block me.

"Awww!" she keened, out of breath. Fear choked her like horrid hiccups. "Awww!"

"I'll kill her, man!" Shotgun shouted.

I tried to kick him but missed. My forty-six careless years slowed me. The flu did not help.

My foot went out again. He dodged my foot, half-lifted her and made it to the curb.

He hauled her into the street.

"Open the door!" he shouted over his shoulder.

I pulled myself to my feet and ran after him.

Behind me, men in tuxedos came through the doorway.

"Stop that animal!" one of them shouted.

"Call 911!"

"My God Almighty!"

"I'll get that gun off him!" yet another bellowed. "Doesn't frickin' scare me."

"You must be nuts," I said. "Where they been hiding you?"

A blue Jeep Cherokee was double-parked on the street. That looked like the getaway car. Black tape masked the numbers.

"Open the door," Shotgun shouted. "Do it! Shoot this fool loser!"

I was this fool loser.

The Jeep backed up, jolted towards me and hit my hip. It knocked me back onto the asphalt. My head went back and smacked the ground.

"Shoot! Shoot!" Shotgun cried out.

The Jeep Driver, wearing a cartoon-green clown mask, swiveled around. He pointed a black semi-auto gun at me.

I rolled backwards, away from that gun.

The Driver gunned the Jeep forward.

"No, goddamnit!" Shotgun shouted. "Wait up!"

The Jeep straightened out and flew down the street. The Driver caught the light on Lexington and was gone.

The girl in the red dress writhed. She tried to break free. A long thigh showed under the skirt. Her blonde hair threaded through wind-whipped snow. She was whimpering now, her eyes unable to get any wider.

I pushed myself up again and fell down on a knee. I remembered my cop days. On other nights, other victims got hurt because I was too slow.

"Not this one, Shotgun," I said.

Shotgun dragged her to my van and slid the side door open. The girl screamed and grabbed the noose. He hit her a solid punch with his left hand. Her head went back. She sagged into the van. He yanked the noose, still attached to the shotgun, from her head and threw it into the van's front seat.

I slopped back up to my feet.

He slid the van's side door shut.

He got behind the wheel.

My leg muscles shaking, I sprang at my van.

He floored the engine.

I tried hooking my left arm around the driver's side mirror.

My van sped up.

I threw a short right strike to his temple. He turned. It hit his ear and skittered off without stopping him.

The van jolted.

The side mirror bent.

I was hanging onto it.

My feet dragged on the roadway.

I lifted them, but they kept dragging. Fear choked me. Every cop's nightmare was getting dragged to death by a speeding perp in a car, using all that metal and chrome to kill. Nothing could stop it. If you shot him dead, his foot would stick on the gas. The car would still drag you until your body broke apart.

He braked.

My legs flew up.

The mirror snapped.

I fell onto the street. My knees smacked the concrete. My nerves screamed. Pain shut my eyes.

The ground hit me again.

I rolled to one side, reaching to my hip for a gun that wasn't there.

There was no van any more.

I opened my eyes.

My van was gone.

Shotgun had taken my van with the girl inside it.

My body lay on the street, aching everywhere

Snow kept falling.

"He kidnapped Huggy!" a man in a tuxedo shouted, coming up to me in the street. "Why did you help him?"

Chapter 2

FUSSING WITH MILLIONAIRES – 5:03 P.M.

"I am not with him," I said. "I delivered the wine, re-member?"

"I damned sure, before God, didn't see that," he said, sputtering. He was the same man who tried grabbing the kid-napper. Blood ran down his head and stained his white collar. His eyeglasses were back on his face. "Now, what I want you to do, sir, is sit over there, do nothing and wait for the authorities."

I sucked in a deep breath and felt all my hurts. I gunned Patrician Eyeglasses with a flat stare, as if he were a pawnbroker without scruples.

"You have heat stroke," I said in a monotone. "But I will call you an ambulance."

Snow swirled between us.

"Is that supposed to be funny?" Patrician Eyeglasses asked. "This is no time for it, sir. I told you to do something. And you had better do it."

"You have heat stroke," I repeated. "But I will call you an ambulance."

He gaped.

"Now, listen –"

"You have heat –"

"All right, all right," he said. "What are you trying to tell me?"

Nerves kept warbling my voice.

"That I am in this," I said. "All the way. Didn't you see me fight him?"

"Thieves fall out. I heard you shout at the driver not to go."

"That was him shouting that, not me."

"Nossir. I remember it as being you."

"You're wrong," I said. "Can you please go down to the corner and stop all traffic from coming here? Re-route them to 72nd Street. Roll a trashcan into the street and block traffic that way."

"You're joking."

"Nossir, I'm not."

My voice trembled.

"I'll fucking do it," said another man, younger and bulkier, and in a tuxedo as well.

Liquor bloomed from his breath.

"You're drunk, Pierce," Patrician Eyeglasses snapped at the younger man.

"No goddamn problem there. But why?"

"To protect the scene," I said. "No pedestrians, either. Don't tell them why. The kidnapper could have his gang watching and listening. Kidnappers usually work in groups. Just pretend you're my Corner Man."

"Oh-Kay!" he said. "Damn!"

He moved to the corner in the whirling snow like it was a football drill. The air grew even chillier. I couldn't see the traffic two blocks away.

"Where did this blizzard come from?" another guest asked. He wore a ceramic Santa Claus pin in his tuxedo lapel and a three-inch scar along his jawbone. "The radio said there would only be flurries."

"Maybe they meant 'Furies'," remarked another.

"You guys," I said.

The old cop lingo thickened my voice as it came back. Two years in Patrol had marked me.

"Whoever has the guts, please get up to Lexington Avenue and block off all pedestrians. Nobody in or out. Tell them that there's a – a hellfire. I don't know."

"A gas leak?" asked Santa Claus Pin.

"Dummy, if there's a gas leak, everyone will want to scoot," another 30-something in a tuxedo said. "Use the gray matter, for dear Heaven's sake."

I tried pulling up a knowing and tolerant grin from the Patrol years.

"Now, boys," I drawled, like the big black Sergeant Borgess had done it in my rookie year.

They reacted to it.

For a second, they were back in their college football years with Coach. They bent their heads to hear wisdom.

"Who went to a good school here?" I asked. "Come on, don't hold your mud."

They looked at each other, grinning secretly.

"Amherst," said one. He stood over me by six inches, his cheeks a rosy red color. His mushroom-colored hair shivered in the wind.

"Wesleyan."

"Yale."

"Well, I'm sure that they taught you to be sneaky," I said. "For your business career. And marriage. Can't you think up something sneaky to lock down that corner?"

They all simpered.

"Sure, we can," the man from Yale said. "Come on. We can scheme together."

"Like old times," said his pal from Wesleyan. He looked hefty and competent, with prematurely gray hair.

"Sir, do you know that your face is all bloody?" the man from Yale asked me

"Yup," I said. "It hurts to talk or move my head. And I got the damn flu."

"The flu is bad this winter."

"Thanks for that news," I said. "Sorry for the wisecrack. Everything's moving too damn fast, you know? Name is Max."

"Preston," the one from Amherst said.

His grip reminded me to exercise more.

"Preston, did you see any of this?"

"Any of the kidnapping, you mean?"

"For starters, yes."

"I heard a commotion. Then this fellow with a stocking mask on was in the front dining room with a big goddamn pistol."

"How big?"

"As large as my forearm," he said.

"Sawed-off shotgun. Cut down a regular shotgun. And you get something incredibly powerful. Kill three victims with one trigger pull before anyone shifts their ass. It's a horrible weapon."

"He had a noose tied around her head," Preston said. "If she tried to knock it away, he would slaughter her. So we all froze. We had to, right?"

"Absolutely," I said.

A woman had stepped over the wine-sodden cardboard and shattered wine bottles to peer at us.

She could peer as much as she wanted, for all of me. She was a pampered beauty, caged in wealth but ready to spring. I hoped that she would take an interest and help us. Long black hair, sleek as sealskin, fell past her shoulders. She stood like a dancer, her long mink coat whipping in the wind above regal thigh boots.

She frowned as she listened to us, her lean, expressive face reflecting the snowglow in the increasing darkness.

"You did the right thing," I told him. "How did he get into that dining room. Do you know?"

"All the brownstones share the garden," Preston replied. "He was shoveling snow when we opened the door. He looked like he belonged there. Any garden members could have hired him to clear the snow off. I mean, who notices someone working that looks like he belongs there?"

"You're right, Preston," I said. "Then what?"

"By the time I got downstairs, everyone was shouting, and he was within twenty feet of the front door. He said that if any of us tried to stop him, he would kill Huggy. So we froze. He yanked open the door and fought with someone, I think."

"He beat me up," I said. "Now, Preston, I need you to do something tough."

"I just want Huggy back, sir."

"Me, too. Start door-knocking all the brownstones in the garden. Do you know any of them?"

"Some."

"That helps. Write down names, addresses and phone numbers. Even if they say that they saw nothing. Swear them to secrecy and tell them the truth. We'll need to talk to them later."

"And you," I said to the Yale man. "Please go inside and separate everyone who saw anything. Put them in the bathroom if you have to."

"Why?" he demanded. "Why?"

He was used to being in charge. Taking orders was a switch for him.

"Because I don't want them contaminating each other's memories," I said. "Independence is best, right?"

He grunted noncommittally.

"If you're too shy to do it, I understand," I said.

He shook his head.

"Shyness has never been my problem," he said. "Consider it done."

He hunched back to the brownstone.

"Excuse me, sir," the woman said. The faintest foreign accent made a burr in her voice. "But what you are doing is wrong. You have no right to order people around."

I stepped back into the chilling wind.

"My name is Max, and I'm asking these people to help. And doing it ever so gently."

Her face formed a study in black. Two coal-colored eyebrows over furious dark eyes echoed her charcoal mane.

"I'm a Free-Thinker and do not approve of how you Americans try to run the world," she said. "It always brings tragedy."

"I'm not trying to turn South Vietnam into Southampton," I said. "Just bring a scared teenager back to her family."

"Wilhelmina Huggins Van Leer needs professional help, yes," she said. "But not from a fat, drunken deliveryman."

"I agree," another tuxedo said, coming out from the brownstone. He took out a cigar case with a shaking hand. "There's something wrong here. I called the FBI, and they're sending someone."

"That will make things worse," she said. "Government intrusion into our private lives."

"Excuse me for halting this Walden Pond dialogue," I said. "But did either of you see any of this happen?"

"I saw it," she said.

"My name is Max," I said. "And if you saw it, you're now my favorite person."

"Zorah DaSilva, Max," she said. "But I'll deal with this is my own way."

"I'd like to know how," I said.

She swept herself and her mink coat back inside the brownstone.

The tuxedo with the shaky hand puffed on a thick cigar that blended with the frosty air. His young face was congealing under blondish hair going gray. His sky blue eyes took me in. His pure white teeth gleamed around the cigar. He stooped a bit for his height, about two inches over mine. A gold wristwatch flashed near an immaculate shirt cuff. His shoes were made of the supple type of black leather that I could never afford.

He put out a cloud of blue smoke. Now his hands stood steady.

"You're taking this over?" he asked me, in the tones of a man that always had time. Nobody hurried him up.

His voice reminded me that I wore a battered leather-and-sheepskin bomber jacket, now stained and reeking with expensive wine, blue flannel shirt, bluejeans and sneakers. That formed my no-snow winter kit. But snow was whipping down fiercely now. I felt like a humble soiled child, and my teeth chewed my bloody lower lip to prove it. New pain flowered.

"For now, sir," I said, falling back into the cop style.

"I'm Cyrus Van Leer," he said, like the President introducing himself at a strip club. Nothing more was needed. "My daughter, Huggy, was the one kidnapped. Who are you, sir?"

"Max Royster."

We shook. His grip felt like he was holding back.

"And do you have any expertise in this, Max?"

"Just common sense, sir."

I could not tell him that I was an ex-cop, fired by Virtue of Mental Disease. He would see me as a suspect. The others were already accusing me.

"There may be skid marks where the getaway Jeep sped up," I said. "Preventing any other cars from covering the marks might help us ID the Jeep. And I've got the pedestrians stopped in case anyone noticed the Jeep driver. And the witnesses separated, I hope."

"I see."

"Mr. Van Leer, what's your business?"

"Oh, various things, Max. Nothing to bore you with."

"Because this kidnapper may know you from business. He chose you for a reason. It may be close to home."

"Really?"

"Are you married?"

"What? "

"To your first wife?" I continued.

"Yes."

"Happily?"

"Max, that's where our talk ends. What official right do you have to ask these questions?"

"I have plenty of right. He kicked me. Tried to kill me with my own van. How does my face look?"

"A bloody mess." He blew out a breath. "You're really infuriating me, you know? He kicked you, but he kidnapped my daughter. What if it were your goddamn daughter?"

"We don't have time for this. I've got to make calls."

"No! You may find me easier to handle than my guests. They include a federal judge, a well-known TV reporter and the Assemblyman for this district. If they want you in prison, they'll find a way to put you there. They run the machine."

"I know," I said. "This is the Upper East Side. Everyone has cash or pretends to. I call it 'the Playpen' because you can live and die here without ever having to grow up."

"Well," he said.

"What you're telling me is that this Christmas party is for the elite," I said. "Everyone has a good future, a better wardrobe, and they all think that they are the cat's ass."

Right on cue, Pierce staggered away from his post.

"Hold that thought," I told Van Leer, as I moved away, I approached the weaving athlete. "Excuse me, there, my Corner Man. Whither are we drifting?"

"It's cold there," he said.

"Yes, 'tis," I said. "Happens every time around this year. Darndest thing I ever did see."

"Oh, and you're a stand-up comic, too?"

"I saw you take that city trashcan and roll it into the street. Those things weigh about three hundred pounds. Otherwise, New Yorkers would steal them for their living rooms. But you handled that like it was paper. Can't you give me some more time on the corner?"

"Okay, okay," he said. "Damn."

He lumbered back to the corner. Snow stuck to his tuxedo.

"Hey, you've got mutiny here," Preston, the witness separator, called from the brownstone doorway.

Van Leer shot me a look saying that he had told me so.

◙

The entrance hall warmth wrapped around me after the sharp chill outside. I felt afraid to go back outside. My body wanted to put on a thick coat, limp upstairs and sleep under three wool blankets. The shiny brownstone floors, with immaculate corners lacking dust or cobwebs, reminded me that I did not belong here. The tasteful wooden furniture and the original oil paintings of New England foliage reinforced this. A fireplace smell from upstairs tickled my nose. Heavy lilac-colored drapes protected the entrance hall windows and prevented anyone on the street from looking inside.

A group of Playpenners in evening dress flowed through a wide swinging door from the kitchen. They looked down their noses at me and made me want to run.

"You don't have any right to do this," a blond All-American-Boy type said to me. Scotch blew from his breath. He stood about my weight but solid as a stone barn. Muscles rippled under his tuxedo. He looked about 25, feisty and angrily drunk.

Fear-sweat wet me.

This was pulling me back into policing again.

I crowded into All-American Boy, bumping him into the foyer wall. That way, he could not use his long-range punches and strength against me. Smart boxers used the ring corners this way.

"Oh, yes, I do," I said.

My left hand came up to my hip level. My fingers spread and tensed.

"Huggy's life is at stake here," I said.

"But you're just abusing this crisis," he said. "I'm going to stop you."

He tried getting off the wall.

My left hand grabbed his testicles and held on.

"One more move," I said, "And I rip and tear."

His right arm moved.

My hand gripped harder.

"Stand down," I whispered. "We can work together. No need for this raw-jaw."

My right fingers touched his lapel and stayed there. I smiled. Anyone watching would see All-American Boy and me as pals.

"That other hand will take out your throat," I said. "I've done this before. To make the rent. But you're an amateur. Don't worry. You'll get your chance at me."

"Now?"

"Now, I win, and you stay in bed for a week. So let's wait a bit, huh?"

I waited.

The blue eyes wavered.

"What's your name?" I asked.

"Christopher. They call me 'Mad Dog'."

"Now, why would they do that?"

I slithered away.

"We're leaving," the beauty named Zorah said. "This is abuse."

The crowd behind her, in tasteful Chesterfield tweeds and furs, agreed.

I took a deep breath. Mad Dog had cost me.

"Sure, you all can leave," I said to them. "But only if you don't care about Huggy."

They grumbled.

"And your own reputations," I went on. "Your own people will talk about tonight for years. You will be known as the ones who left early. To get a good night's sleep. Like some Titanic survivors. People will always gossip and speculate. Do you want that?"

Zorah sat down and glared at me. Some people slid off their coats.

Others copied them.

They were staying.

I sank into a tasteful padded chair.

But it tempted me too much. My leg muscles forced me up and past the paintings and the doorway to go back outside and freeze.

Chapter 3

GUNS AT ME – 5:32 P.M.

A sharkfin Cadillac whipped around the corner from Third Avenue and brushed the trashcan.

The trashcan flew.

My Corner Man Pierce jumped aside. The trashcan tapped his pants leg.

"You got brains in your ass!" he shouted.

The Cadillac whipped up to me.

The driver jumped out. He pointed a silver-plated Magnum at me.

"Freeze! FBI!" he shouted in a New England accent that sounded like President Kennedy gone flat.

My hands snapped up high and empty.

My gut sucked in.

"I'm freezing, I'm freezing," I babbled. "Consider me frozen."

Snowflakes matched his white hair, combed into a crest. He stood a wiry, well-kept six feet in his tuxedo. His face bloomed reddish above the cream-white shirt. Either the cold or excitement gave him that color. His eyes were a skyblue and cold right now. If people were animals, he would be a senior white-haired wolf, running the pack and secure in his power.

In his left hand, he held open a black leather folder, the cards in it stamped with blue-green initials: FBI. His photo showed alongside the initials on the card. He flipped the folder shut. A small gold badge pinned outside winked.

"Move your hands, and I'll take appropriate action," he said.

"Why don't you holster up?" I asked. "That would be an appropriate action."

"Deputy Assistant Director Wilbur Chichak," he said. "You're described as a subject in a kidnapping. What's your name?"

Three more cars streaked around the corner, red police lights flashing on their grilles. Other agents in formal dress leaped out of the cars. They gripped black Glock pistols and gold badges in their mitts.

"FBI! FBI!" they chanted over each other.

I blew out a breath. My body tried to slow itself down as the Magnum barrel pointed at me.

"You've got enough backup here, Special Agent," I said. I demoted him on purpose to distract him. "No need for your gun."

"Keep your hands up and turn around," he said in a steely voice. "Don't reach for anything."

Still shaking, I obeyed.

He stared at my wine-spattered cuffs, and his mouth turned down. That angered me more. Getting dirty was not my idea.

Then his free hand whacked my hips, flanks and pockets. It was a rapid and sloppy frisk. A leather bomber jacket can hide a flat pistol or dagger under the material. In a Brooklyn alleyway, I had learned that lesson the hard way when the client had slashed me across my palm with a Boy Scout pocketknife.

"Now, the gun is secured," he said.

The Yankee accent muted. Maybe it came out only when situations excited him. My New York City accent acted up that same way.

"Tell me who you are, and what you're doing here."

"I'm injured," I said, "and freezing cold. The kidnapper beat me."

"I see that you're hurt."

Time to start lying.

"I have a steel plate in my head."

More likely, I had rocks in there.

"A concussion could kill me. While I'm in your custody, that is."

"You're not in custody. You're helping us of your own volition. And we'll get you treatment."

"Inside your car," I said. "Not out here."

"I'm running this case. Who are you to tell me where you'll talk?"

"Your car is safe from listeners," I said. "The house is not. And anyone could be videotaping us now. That would not help anything. Besides, I'm cold out here."

He chewed this over, his face muscles working.

Some of the agents looked at each other. They were mostly slim and young, like junior executives. All of them, men and women, sported formal wear. This was turning into the night of the tuxedos.

"All right," he said. "I'll make the concession. This once."

ᙯᔆ

As Chichak's agents stared, we settled into the plush velour seats of the old-fashioned Cadillac. I tilted my seat back with the electric buzzer.

"Does Congress know about you buying this showboat?" I asked.

I eased my wallet with my ID out of the back pocket so that he couldn't see my hand move.

"It was confiscated," he said. "Now cut the malarkey and talk."

His broad Yankee "a" soared in the word "mahlahkey."

My fingers closed around my wallet. I stuffed it under the front seat as far as possible. Any second, he might remember that he had felt my wallet during the frisk. He should have remembered already. Maybe he had lost his street smarts. Or maybe he never had them.

"My name is Max, and I delivered Mr. Van Leer's wine tonight. Or I tried to."

I gave him everything except my last name and that I was an ex-cop.

Two NYPD blue-and-white patrol cars rolled up to the corner. Preston, my Tuxedo Assistant, was inside the brownstone warming up. An FBI agent and his Government car blocked the street, red lights flashing. An unmarked car pulled up behind the NYPD cars.

"What gave you the idea to protect the scene and separate witnesses?" he asked.

"I read a lot of cheap detective stories," I said. "Some people think that I even talk like a policeman."

"I'm going to have to insist on you giving us your last name and your background," he said. "You're smart enough to realize that we need that, and then you can go home."

"I've got a traffic warrant for a ticket," I said truthfully. "Maybe."

"Maybe?"

"I'm not real strong on personal paperwork. I may have mailed them the check already. Maybe not. Christmas, you know. So much mailing to do."

"Max –"

His face closed in on mine. That scared me enough to make me step back.

"I'm after a kidnapper. Traffic warrants are not something that concern me. As a federal officer, I can't even act on a local warrant."

"But you could feed me to the locals. Now's a perfect time since they are right here."

The radio crackled in the dashboard.

"Sir," the radio voice said. "The locals insist on speaking with the ranking agent."

"I bet they do," I said.

Chichak sighed and brushed back his pompadour with slim fingers.

"I'll be right there," he said into the radio mike.

And then to me. "Come along, Max. But I'd really feel more comfortable addressing you by 'Mister' and your last name."

"Call me Archduke Ferdinand," I said. "I'll answer to that."

We got out of the car and back into the cold.

CƷ

"This is turning into a real blizzard," Chichak said. "Look at that snow piling up. I'm sure that your family needs you home shoveling the walk and making sure the cars can get out."

"There are more things on heaven and earth," I misquoted "than are dreamt of in all your suburban philosophy."

No family Christmas beckoned to me. A beerbag ex-wife drifting somewhere through West Texas, parents in Miami and my brothers and sisters too wary of me to invite me to their dinners.

I kept my head down and face averted. Some of the NYPD cops might recognize me. I'd worked in the neighborhood before and become reasonably notorious. If they told Chichak, he could use the warrant to jail me and take me out of the action.

We reached the NYPD cars. Chichak approached the driver, a slim black cop with gold-rimmed eyeglasses. He flashed his FBI credentials. The cop yawned in Chichak's face and without wasting a word jerked a thumb at the unmarked car behind him.

Chichak nodded like he wanted to be one of the boys. He swiveled to the unmarked car with credentials out.

The detective driving the unmarked car was a stranger to me. He wore a necklace of chins of fat under his close-shaven jaws. Shrewd piggy eyes took us in. His face was sinking down into those chins.

His muddy hair was almost gone on top. His mouth rolled a DiNobili stogie that once upon a time was the favored cigar of small-time wiseguys. I used to smoke them myself. I had not seen them for years. The smell covered all of us.

Easy listening elevator music blended with the NYPD radio.

"All units," the radio said. "Winter storm warning in effect."

The detective's passenger was a chunky Latina woman with dyed blonde hair and a rhinestone necklace tucked into her raincoat. She was chewing gum religiously.

— 24 —

"I'm Chichak of the FBI."

Chichak did not think me worth introducing.

"We've got an active kidnapping here on this street. We're taking over the entire case. And the responsibility. No local help is needed, thank you very much."

"One-Nine Squad David," the detective said, no expression at all in his flat, city-accented voice. "Report of a past kidnap. Suspect fled in hijacked van, gone by twenty minutes ago. Weapon seen, shotgun. Pro-ceed."

Nobody moved.

"Did you hear what I said?" Chichak asked. "Are you messing with me.?"

"Ten-four. 'kay," the detective said in the same monotone. "We'll take that call."

Only a cop would know what he was doing. He was reciting the radio call as a kind of relaxation mantra. Old- timers, the kind that we called "hair bags," did it all the time.

They used it to get to sleep after rough nightmarish nights. Most hair bags seemed half-asleep while working.

"I'm in charge of the entire case," Chichak said. "Deputy Assistant Director. We are relieving you of all responsibility on this one."

"Central, be advised," the detective said, "that federal agents, the crack elite team of law enforcement worldwide, is already on the scene and expects an arrest forthwith."

Nothing moved in the detective's broad doughy face. He sounded like he was addressing a child or an idiot.

"Detective whoever you are," Chichak said. "This is a federal crime scene. Inside a millionaire's brownstone. I don't want you sticky-fingered cops picking up souvenirs because the city underpays you. You know that it happens, and so do I. But not tonight. I have my own reputation and case to protect."

The detective looked Chichak over and eased the car back into traffic, the patrol cars following him. The slim black cop dumped a coffee cup out the window.

CB

Chichak and I walked back towards Van Leer's brownstone.

"My cellphone is out of service," I said. "I couldn't pay the bill. Christmas, right? Loan me yours to call my lawyer. If he says okay, I'll get all undressed for you. Deal?"

"Why all this cooperation all of a sudden?" Chichak asked.

"Maybe like you said. I want to go home."

"I don't know."

"Eliminate me as a suspect, and you can make real progress on your case. Tell you what. I'll let you listen in. Anything wrong, you stop the call."

"I can't listen to you talk to your lawyer."

"You can if I let you. Come on, Deputy Assistant Director. Before I think twice about it."

"Okay."

He passed me his cellphone. He was thinking that his phone memory would give me the lawyer's number and name.

I punched in a number.

"Put it on speaker, please," Chichak said. He gripped my wrist holding the phone.

"3747," a man's deep voice said.

"This is Max calling for a David Balfour situation here," I said. "Find my work van. David's inside the van-"

Chichak wrested the phone from me and spoke into it.

"This is Deputy Assistant Director Wilbur Chichak, of the FBI New York Field Office. What law firm is this, please?"

"It's not," the deep voice said. "It's an answering service."

"For which attorney?"

"Many lawyers, sweetheart. Too many for my particular taste."

"This man who called you, what's his name?" Chichak asked, his accent coming back.

"Cupcake, why don't you ask him yourself? You sound very forceful and masculine."

"What's your name?"

"Myron, sweets."

"Your last name?"

"Are you looking for a date, sweets? I'm shaken to the tits."

"I've got your number. I can subpoena your records and arrest you for Interfering with a Federal Officer in the Performance –"

"Excuse me, sweets. My other line is ringing. Call me later for that date."

The call ended.

Chichak glared.

He looked like he wanted to slug me.

"Who is this David Balfa you talked up?" he asked. "What's that about?"

"Not now," I said. "Should I tell your wife about you and Myron?"

"Now, goddamnit! I could arrest you right now," Chichack said.

Car doors slammed. Agents jumped into their cars.

"Boss!" one shouted. "Radio!"

Chichak whirled. He leapt to his Cadillac and ripped open the door.

"All units," his radio said. "I've got the kidnap vehicle in sight. He's speeding southbound on Park Avenue at Seven-Three Street. Any unit, come in."

Chichak hit the ignition. I jumped into the passenger seat.

We roared away.

Chapter 4

RAIDING – 6:07 P.M.

Chichak handled his Cadillac like a pro, steering out of skids on the snow-covered streets.

I gripped the seatbelt strap. Hollywood usually depicted cops dying in massive assault rifle shootouts. But most actually died in traffic accidents. That bothered me right now.

"The subject is now northbound on Madison and Seven-Two Street," the chasing agent said in a monotone.

"Who is that voice?" Chichak asked aloud. "I know it but I can't place it. The Manual says that he must identify himself throughout the pursuit."

"Unfortunately," I said, "he can't run this pursuit and read the manual at the same time."

"Now east on Seven-Eight," the unknown agent said. "Traffic is light, so I'll hang back. I don't want him to make me tailing him."

Chichak jumped the traffic signal. He switched the channel on his radio.

"New York Base, this is New York 12," Chichak said. "Can we get an airship up?"

"Negative, New York 12," a woman's city accent came through the radio. "All airships are down due to weather."

"New York 2267, I'm joining in the pursuit," a Midwestern voice said.

"New York 1895, ditto," another voice said.

"They're breaking off stakeouts to join us," Chichak said. "I don't want too many. Can't control them."

"Bolshoi," I said. "If he starts running or shooting, you'll need everybody."

"He's going south on Second Avenue again," the unknown agent.

"Agent on the subject, identify yourself," Chichak asked.

Our car slewed around another skid. All my hurts felt it. They sang out whenever my body moved. Having the flu did not help things.

Another FBI car raced up snowy Park Avenue, just missed our fender and turned east towards Lexington Avenue.

"Everybody, just cool it," Chichak said over the radio. "I don't want any paperwork on accidents."

On cue, a gypsy cab sped in front of us and spun out. Chichak muttered a gerund as he dodged the cab.

"Every damn fool with a cab is raring around to make that last buck before hibernating through this storm," I said.

"When did you drive a cab, Max?"

I smiled.

"You won't get my resume that easily, Mr. Chichak."

"The title is Deputy Assistant Director."

"I can shorten that to D-A-D," I said. 'So you can be my dad, and I'll play the rebellious teenager."

Chichak jetted the car past another cab.

Two other cars, probably FBI, flashed in front of us.

"All units," the unknown agent said. "Subject is a male, race unknown, taking a woman, red dress, inside 338 East Six-Five Street. Van just dropped them."

"Huggy, the victim is wearing a red dress," I said. "Velvet."

"Description of the subject?" Chichak snapped over the radio.

"They're inside now," the unknown said. "I'm going off the air."

"Agent on the subject, identify yourself," Chichak said. "Or else, I end this pursuit."

The radio was silent.

"Who's on that street?" Chichak asked.

Nobody answered.

"It's just up there," I said.

"When I get there, you stay in the car," Chichak said. "You're still a subject."

He parked on Second Avenue, threw on a tweed overcoat from the back seat and went out into the snowstorm.

65th Street was right ahead. I knew the block, like I knew most blocks in the Playpen.

Another car parked behind me. Two FBI junior executive types, tuxedos under their raincoats, moved past me.

The wind howled again.

Chichak returned to the car, bringing chill air and a flurry of flakes with him when he got in. Snow already dusted his shoulders.

"This is turning into a winter nightmare," I said. "The storm will help the kidnapper escape, whether or not he kills Huggy."

Chichak shot me a harsh look, crafted to make me feel like an underling. He spoke into his radio mike.

"First, two agents to cover the back of the brownstone," he said. "Get as close as you can. Don't anybody bunch up. Play it loose. If he has her in that brownstone, he's not getting away. Runyon, meet me on the corner, please."

That word "please" made me grin. Chichak was showing his kids that a true gentleman could stay suave under pressure.

Runyon bobbed up from the snow storm. He was black, about 25 and looked like a comic book action hero, his eyes hiding a smirk behind his respectful face. He seemed like a team player who would come through in the clutch.

Women would swoon over him. They would step over me to get near him.

"Runyon, we need to get inside there without a ruckus," Chichak said. "He could still have that shotgun wired to her head."

Runyon nodded.

"Yeah, okay," was all that he said.

He padded down the street.

"Strong, silent type," I said.

"Max, can you turn down the wisecracks?" Chichak said. "Just because you don't believe in anything. Some of us still do."

Runyon approached the three-story brownstone. I hoped that it was the right one. The doors and windows were done in dark wood paneling. It looked like a castle that no barbarian could hope to storm.

My knees bent. I wanted to get inside with Runyon, backing him up with my nightcrawling experience and Glock NYPD service gun.

The brownstone jutted out a bit from the façades of the other buildings on the block. All the windows that I could see were dark. It did not look as if anyone were inside.

Runyon stood on a metal fence that extended from the brownstone's door. He reached as high as he could. Snow made him wobble. He bent his knees and vaulted up as high as he could.

One hand caught the top of a window sill on the first floor. The sill had an ironwork design under the snow.

Runyon strained. One foot went against the wall and wedged him further up the brownstone's facade. Like a trapeze expert, he moved up to the second-floor window and chinned himself up to the window sill.

Then he was lost from sight.

"That's amazing," I said. "I could never do that."

"I know," Chichak said. "For many reasons."

"How can he climb like that?"

"He volunteered and did it twice before on brownstones. Sometimes he fails. But he can do what others can't."

Chichak picked up a throat mike that I had not seen before. His voice was pitched so low that it was hard to hear him.

"Runyon, your job is to get inside and then let us in," he said. "Don't play cowboy on me."

"Roger," Runyon breathed back.

"It's driving me cuckoo," I said. "But why are all of you dressed in tuxes and formal dresses?"

"The U.S. Attorney's Office held its holiday ball tonight. Black tie. They granted us an award for excellence."

We drifted towards the front of 338. Chichak opened his topcoat and reached a hand back towards his right hip. That silver-plated Magnum would be resting there in a holster.

Other agents spread out behind us, their faces tense. They had their coats open or pockets bulging.

The front door opened.

A gold FBI badge came out in Runyon's big hand. He was shrewd enough to identify himself without noise, to keep anyone from shooting him by mistake.

Other agents rushed inside without a sound.

"We've got him cornered now," another agent said behind me.

"Hush up," Chichak whispered. "He could be listening."

The wind picked up again.

Snow was coming down harder now and spinning into drifts. Only a few cabs inched down Second Avenue. Their windshield wipers tried batting the thick snow back off the glass.

"Let's stay inside," I told Chichak. "Someone may be watching this place."

"Do you think so?"

"And it's colder than a well-digger's dump."

A woman agent, dark-skinned and short, came to the front door. She carried a red-beamed flashlight between her silk party dress and her raincoat.

"Empty, boss," she said. "Nobody home."

Chichak shook his head.

"Are you sure?" he asked.

"We checked everywhere. Nobody has been in here for days. Probably left for the holidays."

"Then who broadcast?"

The other agents came down into the front of the brownstone.

The speaker on Chichak's throat mike buzzed.

"It was an old Bureau tradition," a man's voice said over the speaker. "Whenever an agent embarrassed the Bureau, he would resign. I embarrassed us all tonight. Tell Mr. Hoover I did my best."

Chichak and the other agents froze.

"Whose voice is that?" one agent asked.

"That's the question of the night," I said. "Because J. Edgar has been graveyard dead for a long time. One of you has cracked up. And we don't know who."

Chapter 5

PEP TALK – 6:41 P.M.

The agents clustered around Chichak as the snow swirled around them. It made me feel isolated and alone. They had their club, and they kept me out of it.

"All right," Chichak said. "Back inside. We'll hold a debrief now."

"Right now?"

Chichak gave them a tolerant smile, like a firm but loveable housemaster in some prep school.

"I don't need to remind you all," he said, "veterans or baby agents, how valuable a debrief can be. But to have much value, it should be right after the activity. Otherwise, memories fade, perceptions change, and we lose the full teaching value of the debrief. And remember that the Bureau is a thinking man's game. We outthink these criminals whenever possible. Let the local cops have the gunfights, car chases, liabilities, civilian complaints and high profile. We'll just complete our investigations and imprison subjects, when necessary."

A Latino agent with a handlebar moustache pointed at me. "Sir, do we need this person here?"

"He's already seen and heard the whole raid," Chichak said. "Now, we've all gone through the course at the Academy on Raiding Structures. This brownstone here is no different.

First, when we got the address, I asked for two agents to cover the back. Who did it and how?"

"Sir, Markeloy and Veds," a rail-thin agent with reddish hair said. "I'm Markeloy. It was impossible to cover the back of 338 from East 64th. But there is an all-night restaurant, the Silver Moon, on that corner. We thought that they might have an egress to the 338 area. So we entered the restaurant, showed our creds, and the manager led us through the kitchen to the walkway outside. Agents Wetzel and York watched our flank. We were able to be physically close to 338's rear in case a subject exited."

"That's thinking, all right," Chichak said. "Runyon, what was your sighting once inside the house?"

Runyon's thick body heaved inside the tuxedo. His tea-colored eyes roved over the group of agents. Up close now, he looked even younger. He might be 23 or 24, with little life experience outside the Bureau. This would be his first real job. His face and manners said that he would do whatever he was told to do.

"Sir, I first had to make sure that the subject and victim were not inside the home," he said. "I stayed quiet and listened. There was nothing. A possible ambush was my main concern. Our subject had used violence and a death threat during the initial kidnap. So I did not want to take any unnecessary risks.

"I went from the window area where I entered, drew my issued Glock and listened again. Everywhere that I could, I switched on lights. The bathroom sinks had no wet spots on them. The beds had not been slept in recently. There was no sign that anyone had been living there. So I went downstairs to the front door and opened it for you all to enter."

"Sir, what about this agent broadcasting, this 'Crackup'?" another agent asked from the back of the group. He was too far back in the shadows for me to see him.

"I'm not going to speculate on that issue at this time," Chichak said. "It may be a one-time lapse, never to be repeated again. Someone may have fallen off his medications for tonight alone. A bank robber mortally wounded Special Agent Baker, and Baker's last words were, 'Tell Mr. Hoover I did my best.' Every agent knows that story. We have a fresh kidnap tonight with a live victim and many tasks to perform. We cannot play Dr. Freud along the way. I know you'll do your best to save the victim."

"But, sir, we're in a victim-hostage situation here. Shouldn't we know?" the Latino agent said.

"Can we know?" Chichak asked. "New York Field Office has about 1100 agents. Each has a radio. This broadcast could come from any one of them. At this time of night, with our Tech Support people at home, there is no way to track that transmission. So let's just carry on our primary mission, all right? Wetzel, York, Smelka, Evers, and you all, do we agree?"

The agents shifted their positions. To me, they did not look satisfied.

"And, if we make too much of this now," Chichak went on, "Washington gets involved. You know what that means. They will take us off this case within the next hour, order us to surrender our issue handguns pending psychiatric testing and assign us to in-house clerical work until those tests are completed. Ladies and gentlemen, that is how the Bureau avoids lawsuits in case one of us goes haywire and shoots an innocent. But it is NOT how we crack kidnappings."

"Nobody wants Washington involved," the Latino agent agreed.

"From those wonderful people who helped bring us the World Trade Center," Markeloy muttered.

"What?" I said. "What do you mean?"

"I'm going to pretend that I did not hear that," Chichak said. He gave another housemaster smile. "A moment's unwise comment should not mar anyone's career record. But let me remind you that as a Deputy Assistant Director, I am privy to most of your medical records. And if I am down-playing this issue of 'the Crackup', as you deem fit to call him, it may be for a good reason. And you may not know that reason yet."

Chichak took a step forward to his group. It looked as if the housemaster had controlled his schoolboys.

"If there are no further items, this debrief is over," he said. "I'll want two agents to stay here until the homeowners can be contacted in the morning. See Mr. Runyon for that assignment."

Chichak moved over to me. The agents retreated back to their cars, snow hitting their evening dress.

"Chichak, you tell them to ignore the Crackup, and they just do it?" I asked. "That never would happen in real life."

"Hmmm."

"Or maybe your Bureau is not real life."

"Max, what do you know about the Bureau?"

"More with each minute."

"Then you should know that we are different from other Government agencies," he said. "Our discipline is strict. Some call it intolerable. Agents who can't deal with it usually resign within a few years and write wildly inaccurate diatribes against us. But agents must obey all orders coming from their bosses. If they do not, they are dismissed. It is that simple. It is the only way to conduct the complex and multifaceted investigations that we do."

"I think that you need a union," I said.

"That kind of thinking demonstrates why you could never be one of us."

Agent Markeloy brought Cyrus Van Leer over from a Crown Victoria sedan.

"Mr. Van Leer," Chichak said, "we escorted you to this location in case your daughter was here."

"Actually, you might have needed me to identify her body," Van Leer said.

His voice drooped, his head following.

"You may not know this," Chichak said, "but the Bureau has an excellent record in resolving kidnaps with the victim returned safely, and the subjects apprehended. And the money, if any, recovered. We stand by that reputation."

"That's a comfort."

"Yes, sir. Now, you said that Max here told you his last name. Can you remember what that was?"

My knees bent. I wanted to run or hit something. If Van Leer remembered my name, then Chichak could run my name and come up with all kind of information on me. He would then drop me into a cell on a charge of making the FBI lose their Walt Disney smiles or some such nonsense. I would be off this case.

Van Leer scrunched up his face. Then he shook his head.

"No," he said. "I'm afraid that I can't. Not right now. But I know me. The name will come back to me sometime tonight. Trust me."

My body loosened. My head went back against the tight shoulder muscles. Markeloy led Van Leer back to the car.

"There's a father in torment," Chichak said. "And I'm afraid that you're adding to it."

"I don't want to. I want to get Huggy back to him."

"You, alone? And bypass the FBI? That's a fantasy, Max."

"I'll be glad to work with you."

"Then start now. Give us your data, and let us go after the true criminals here. Not the wisecracking immature bystander that I feel you to be. Harmless but delaying our central mission."

"Mr. Chichak, that debrief just showed me something about your outfit. You do not control your cases. Washington cuts you orders. And you must follow them. Or, as you say, get fired. So, I'm going to do this my way. Let me be the bad guy. I'll make my own decisions about how to get Huggy back. And that's your best protection. I won't involve you in disobeying your rules."

"Slicksters like you sometimes wind up doing life sentences in federal prisons," he said. "I'm warning you."

"Chichak, what did that agent mean by saying that Washington helped bring us the World Trade Center?" I asked.

"That's not for someone like you to know about," he said. "We've talked enough. I have work to do."

Chapter 6

HOOVER WORSHIP – 7:13 P.M.

The agents stayed out on the snowy sidewalk in front of the brownstone. Christmas lights winked down the block.

Some agents wore raincoats or topcoats to protect their tuxedos. The women wore thickset coats for protection against the weather. But even despite the layers of clothing, I could smell the sweat from their search for the kidnapper. Glock guns showed in belt holsters next to their cummerbunds.

"I never heard of any of us cracking up like this," Evers, the black woman agent, said. Her dark face, thin frame and white lace dress stood out among the other agents.

"Booze, call girls, even suicide. But not Hoover worship," she finished.

"Hoover ran our Bureau single-handedly from 1924 to 1972," another agent said, "and did exactly what he wanted to do during that time."

He looked like a college literary major with the innocent face of someone who devoured libraries and memorized poems. I could not see him wrestling a streetfighting hoodlum into handcuffs.

"Everyone knows that, Smelka," retorted Evers. "It's in the history books."

"What is NOT in the books is that before Hoover took over, our Bureau was a disgrace." Smelka continued. "Nobody wanted to admit that they worked there. But he put in standards, fired whomever he wanted to, manipulated the media and made us the proudest and most famous detective agency in the history of the world."

"Sounds like you love him, Smelka. Maybe YOU made those radio calls."

Smelka blushed.

"J. Edgar Hoover has been dead a long time," another said, taking off his coat over the tuxedo. The gold FBI badge gleamed on the belt clip next to his holster.

"So has Hitler," Evers said. "But little kids will still grow up worshipping what they stood for."

"Hoover was a dictator," the Latino agent said. "All you had to tell the man was 'I'm one of your obedient sons, sir. I will not choke it, poke it or smoke it. I'm dedicated'."

"That's wandering far afield," the tallest agent said in a heavy voice. He stood over me, watery eyes in a neutral face that showed nothing. "It's time for us to think career survival here tonight."

"Why career survival, Levin? What's up with that?"

Levin, the big guy, pointed a thumb at me. "First, maybe we should get rid of this rat listening in."

My breath blew out.

Chichak trudged up the steps to the brownstones.

The agents dutifully followed him

I followed the agents, cheered to get warm again.

CঙS

Fifteen minutes later, we were inside the empty brownstone's foyer, decorated in an Oriental fashion, with knurled wooden furniture and a collection of Asian tapestries on the tan walls. Chichak was working his cellphone, churning out words with the night shift U.S. Attorney's lawyer.

"It's cold outside, Levin," I said. "Besides, nobody wants to watch me when they have a debrief with you."

Levin glowered.

"Big talkers like you get hurt," he said. "Permanently."

"Come on, Levin," Evers said. "Me and Diascu here want to know why you're sweating career survival."

— 40 —

"I was covering the back of the brownstone," Diascu said.

He would be a perfect surveillance agent. Medium height, not fat, not thin, a mild face under tortoise-shell glasses made him hard to remember.

"Agents Wetzel and York were alongside me," he continued. "So I may have missed the good stuff."

"Here it is," Levin said. "The guests at this party are real big shots. You all saw that jewelry. Caught some of those names. If they make a phone call on you, you'll be chasing Army deserters in the Point Barrow Alaska Field Office."

"Why should they?" Diascu asked.

"Because they're now involved up to their moneybelts as seeing a kidnap of this moneybag's kid Muffy, that's frickin' why. And one of us going bonkers is probably going to get the girl killed. I mean, you can't work two things at once. Chichak has to bring this Muffy number back alive AND weed out our cuckoo bird, without any outsider hearing about it."

"So?" Evers said. "He can do it."

"Chichak? He's burnt out. He's been fooling the Bureau these last two years. All he can do is retire. Or get us all jammed up by these rich folks."

"You're always so cheery, Levin," Evers said. "Mister Positive."

"I'm just telling you. Life is crud. You do it to them before they stick it to you."

"So what's the plan?" Diascu asked.

"The plan is, lie, fly and deny," Levin said. "We didn't hear that squirrel on the radio. It could have been a mixed channel from another FBI office. Radio waves skip. That happens at night sometimes. You get Boston or Providence FBI radio calls."

"But we know that it was one of us, right?"

"Sure," Levin said. "And if the Bureau asks, naturally, we tell the truth."

"Nat-turally," someone said in a high-pitched city accent. A chuckle spread.

"Naturally," Levin went on. "But we don't breathe a word to any civilian. Nothing. We keep this all in-house."

"Mum's the word," Evers agreed.

The other made boardroom sounds of approval.

Chichak came downstairs from the second floor, folding his silver-edged cellphone.

"The AUSA wants two agents remaining here until the homeowner can be notified in the morning," Chichak told his agents. "Otherwise, they might claim that things are missing."

"Sure," Diascu said. "I went through college, law school, New Agents' Training at Quantico so I could steal ashtrays from millionaires."

"How does that make you feel, Runyon?" Chichak asked. "You train, stay in shape, risk your life to save a victim, and they stand ready to accuse you of pilfering."

Runyon simpered.

"They always put it on a brother," Evers said. "When they can't find a sistah."

"If there's no further items, this debrief is over."

"Now that you mention it," Diascu smiled his shy grin, "we will be getting hungry soon."

"Got pizza coming," Chichak said. "The Bureau thinks of everything."

Chichak's smile died when he spotted me.

He opened the door and thumbed me towards his Cadillac.

"I could have left when your squad was searching the home," I said as we walked down the brownstone steps.

The snow had been made slippery by the feet of the agents. I worried about falling.

"You try it and they'll land on you like a football team," Chichak said. "You're not free to leave."

"Then I'm under arrest?"

We arrived at his Cadillac. He opened the passenger's side with an old-fashioned key.

"Just get in the car," Chichak said. "Don't try talking like some jailhouse lawyer."

Chapter 7

What I Got to Do – 7:49 P.M.

We drove back towards Van Leer's house, where the agents were keeping passing cars away from each corner.

"The kidnapper has messed up," Chichak said. "He must know that by now. His getaway car and driver took off."

"You mean the getaway got away?" I asked.

Chichak gave me a "Stop it" look.

"He was forced to take a strange car and drive and control the victim AND evade cops, and he still has not made a ransom demand yet. Maybe because he has already killed her. Huggy could be dead right now."

"Adult victims don't usually live as long as kids do," I said. "The kidnapper cannot survive a live victim pointing him out in court."

"You seem to know about this," Chichak said.

"I know more things that don't make me any money than anyone I can name," I said.

"Then know this," Chichak said. "If Huggy is found dead now, I'm saving the Bureau's rep and my own career by putting you in federal prison for life."

My knees came together in the gradually warming Cadillac. My head went back against luxury headrest. The flu made the bump hurt more.

"On what charge?" I asked.

"Accessory before the fact in a kidnap-murder," he said. "With a rich dead victim and a raft of witnesses blaming you, I can get you convicted quite easily."

"And you think I'm helping to kidnap a teenage girl for cash?" I asked.

"I think that you're not cooperating. What other possible motive could you have?"

"If I cooperate, as you call it, you'll stash me in a cell on some imaginary charge," I said. My voice rose. "Then I'm out of the picture. Off the set. Your kidnapper will get away. Or kill Huggy. Or both. And then you'll still have me. So, you're forcing me to do something, Wilbur."

"What's that?"

"You're forcing me to find Huggy for you," I said. "Without gun, respect or power. Or else I'll still wind up in federal prison. So, I've got to."

"Come on," he said. "We're wasting time."

೮೩

Painfully, I hauled my bruises and flu body out of the car and back into the cold. The wind cut my neck. My bruises throbbed again.

Inside the brownstone, the guests looked at me like

I was a bum in wet and dirty clothes. Their faces hardened, making me scared again. This was getting real risky for me.

Runyon sketched the brownstone and labeled each room. I looked at the sketch and tried to memorize it.

Van Leer's brownstone looked different to me now. Any minute now, Chichak could snap his fingers and order me into lock-down. This could be the last Playpen party that I ever crashed.

With that in mind, I stopped by the first floor kitchen, poured myself a hearty Knob Creek and filched some hummus hors d'oeuvres.

"Huggy's poor sister," Zorah the Brazilian beauty was telling my friend Preston, the one from Amherst. "How do you wash away a night like this?"

"Really," Preston said, rolling the word as he said it.

They melted back upstairs.

The kitchen smelled of cooked goose and roasted potatoes. Off to the side, a small sound system played Handel's *Water Music*.

"Here we go," I said, trying to get it up for what I had to do. "I'm back on the street again."

A loose fringe of the Beautiful People was still ranging around the kitchen and the first floor. I finished the hummus, built another drink and accosted Patrician Eyeglasses near the doorway.

I held up the drink as an explanation.

"Excuse me, sir," I said. "But I'm supposed to bring this drink to Huggy's sister."

"Yes?"

Apparently he was not in the "Suspect-Ole-Max-of-Everything" cadre.

"And it's the darndest thing," I said. "I can't seem to find her."

"She's right there by the fireplace," he said. "In the green dress."

"Thank you so much," I said.

He stepped away. He was probably thinking that good domestics were very hard to get.

The fire crackled and snapped in the generous stone fireplace. The heat waves moved the Christmas decorations on a nearby wall.

The girl in the green dress had Huggy's blonde hair, but, she was thicker and shorter and looked about 20. Her blue eyes hopscotched around the room, reminding me of other suspects acting that way in my cop days.

"I'm so sorry," I said, sliding over near her. "They keep telling me your name and it goes right out of my head."

"Bess."

"And they told me, 'Max, make sure that Bess gets this cocktail.' Is it okay with you?"

She stepped back. The green dress went in around her spreading middle. She stood about five foot five inches, average height, but was nearing 135 or 140 pounds. That would make life tough for her in the Playpen, where everyone was supposed to be as slim as a steak knife.

"Who told you to bring me this?" she asked, making a face.

"Now, let me see," I said, trying to clown. "I can narrow it down. It was a white guy."

"Really?"

"And in a tuxedo," I said. "Can you imagine that?"

"He must be a frickin' dweeb of some kind. Everyone knows that I drink Stoly. Nothing else. Still."

She drank some of the bourbon. We could hear the guests speaking to each other upstairs.

"Now that you mention it, he did seem a bit like the dweebish type," I said. "But now I have to talk privately with you. I'm here as kind of a liaison with my FBI buddies."

"You're an FBI man?"

"No, no. Can't be. I'm not skinny enough. I'm just a city character working on a job as a favor before Christmas. Can you tell me what happened with your sister getting kidnapped?"

"I wasn't anywhere near her."

"Okay."

"I mean, it was like –"

She knit her brows trying to think. She drank again.

"He came in through the front door with the guests. They were ahead of him, and he just walked in behind them. He pulled down this stocking thing over his head and grabbed my sister around the neck."

"Did you see any gun then?"

Bess sighed. She shifted her heavy body to one side and looked at the painting of a rural landscape on the wall. A freckle-sized scar showed on the inside of her left wrist. She shook her hands and looked around the room again. The glass went up and down again. The bourbon was almost gone.

Handel's music kept playing out.

I leaned against the counter. My body cried out for bed, thick blankets and twelve hours of sleep. I could sleep through this flu.

"I don't really remember," she said. "Does it matter? We all saw it later. We sure as God saw it."

"And you saw him come inside the front door?" I asked. That clashed with what I had heard earlier, about the kidnapper shoveling snow in the garden and coming in that way.

"Max, are you going to get her back, okay? Because we're really close. We never fight or anything. Get along real well."

"Talking like this helps get her back," I said. "Dumb as it seems, the more info we get, the better this gets for everybody."

Special Agent Diascu stepped into the room, saw us and started to walk away. His milk-fed clear expression pinked a bit.

"Miss, I'm Linc Diascu with the FBI," he said. "Could I borrow Max for a minute here?"

She did not have to think about that. I was no fun to talk to. And she was a girl who liked her fun.

"Okay," she said. "I'll be up on the second floor. With the guests."

She went out, still holding the cocktail that I had given her.

⋈

"What are you doing with her?" Diascu asked.

It was time to play dumb.

"Just talking," I said. "You guys won't let me do anything else. And I've got the flu."

Diascu stepped away. He did not want to catch the flu from me. Nobody did in Christmastime New York. I felt like the Village Leper.

"You stay away from her," Diascu said. "She is the victim's sister."

"Is she? I didn't know that. Sorry. We were just talking about the Hamptons and things. Nothing pertinent."

Diascu's face smoothed out.

"Okay, then. But no more," he said. "In fact, I'd like you upstairs in the living room where most of us are."

The phone rang. The bell sound went throughout the brownstone.

"Don't touch it," Diascu said. "It could be the kidnapper."

Chapter 8

FUMBLING THE BALL – 8:23 P.M.

The phone rang again.

I whirled from the kitchen into the dining room. Runyon stood near the phone, talking to Preston. Chichak came in from the hallway.

"Runyon!" Chichak hissed. "You know the drill!"

"What?" Preston asked Runyon. "Me?"

His voice covered Chichak's words.

The phone rang again.

Chichak's face flushed.

"Runyon!" he shouted. "Get it, boy!"

Runyon froze. So did I.

Calling a black man "boy" was considered very bad table manners. Knife fights had started over far less.

Chichak whipped his head and showed his white teeth against the red skin. Lines grooved his face. He would look this way at eighty.

"Great time for a side issue," I said.

The phone rang again.

I lunged for the phone.

"It's the kidnapper!" a man shouted from upstairs. It sounded like Van Leer.

Preston got there first.

He snagged the phone.

His eyes lit up under the mushroom-colored hair.

"Van Leer residence," he said.

He was doing it just right. But I was moving up on him.

"Give me that!" I hissed.

Chichak was too far away.

Preston extended the phone to me.

A man's voice came from the phone.

I shook my head.

It was too late to switch voices. The kidnapper might hang up. I returned the phone to him.

Preston grinned. He looked as if Coach was handing him the football for the goal kick.

"I'm sorry, sir, I didn't hear you," he said into the mouthpiece.

His elbow swung back. It hit the phone. His grin died. The phone tumbled off the desk.

"Goddamnit!" Chichak shouted.

The phone hit the floor. It gave off a ring and stayed still.

Preston was still holding the handset.

"He's gone," he said. "Just a – just a dial tone."

Van Leer rushed in from the hall.

"You screwed it!" he snapped. "How could you do that? I mean, just what was in your mind?"

"I'm sorry, sir," Preston said. He dipped his head.

"Don't you realize who that was?"

"If I can do anything," Preston said. Now he sounded like a preppy addressing his housemaster.

"What else COULD you do?" Van Leer cracked back.

"Runyon," Chichak said. "We need to speak right now."

Runyon's face looked frozen in time. His mouth stayed open.

"I did not mean anything racial by that," Chichak said.

"Is this necessary right now?" Van Leer asked. "I mean, really."

Runyon just held his ground, head tucked down. He had not moved from his position when the phone had sounded.

Other agents and guests crowded in from the hallway.

I could smell the wood smoke fragrance from the fireplace.

Evers stepped closer, her white lace dress molded to her. The crowd heard Van Leer's tone and saw his face. In the Playpen, locals never used that vocal timbre.

"Come on, Runyon," Chichak tried pulling up a sick smile from somewhere. "You know that every football fight song has the word 'boy' in it."

"I don't know any songs like that," Levin said from the staircase. He smirked, enjoying the scene.

"Growing up in the suburbs," Runyon said. "I didn't know I was black until I joined the Bureau."

"I'm going to sue you, Preston," Van Leer said.

I knew that catch in his voice from Patrol. It meant fighting.

"But first I'm going to tell everyone just what you are," Van Leer continued.

"Man," Evers breathed. "The more money you white people got, the sillier you act."

I was poised and on point for once.

Van Leer rushed for Preston, hands working to grab or punch. I stepped in, slammed my hip into Van Leer and re-directed him down onto a chair against the wall. He hit and bounced back up. I palmed his chest, shoved him down again and stepped in closer.

Preston kept his head tucked down. His tuxedo chest heaved. Tears wet his healthy face.

"You're standing on my feet," Van Leer squawked.

"That's the idea. Don't use them now. If you get up again, I'll forget the strain that you're under. I'll take action that you and your insteps will not like. Clear?"

"Stop that!" Chichak said.

"You handle your own mess, DAD," I said. "We don't need a hissy-fit catfight between millionaires right now."

Chichak stepped closer to me.

"How does it feel to be falsely accused and be innocent?" I asked him.

Chichak made a low noise in his throat and stepped away.

"Runyon, you were supposed to take that call," Chichak said. "Why didn't you?"

"I don't know," Runyon said. Words came out slowly from somewhere deep in him. "I guess that I didn't understand your order."

"This could cost us the case," Chichak said. "Irretrievable setback. And all these outsiders watching. This gives me no pleasure, Runyon, but I'm going to have to put this on paper."

"I understand," Runyon said.

"I don't," I said, still keeping Van Leer down. "The kidnapper may call back in two minutes. Work other angles on the case, Chichak. You can spank the schoolboys afterwards."

Chichak ignored me. Most adults did.

"Neglect of duty," he said. "But I'll do the best that I can for you."

"Of course, sir," Runyon said. "Bureau."

"Bureau," Chichak said. It sounded like a motto when they said it.

"Chichak doesn't have to do that," Diascu said. "For heaven's sake, that could kill Runyon's career."

"Or end it," Evers said.

"They could ship him off to investigate Fair Housing loan violations in Northern Maine," Diascu said. "Real fulfilling work."

"You, Max. Whatever-the-hell your name is," Chichak said. "Get away from Mr. Van Leer. Or I'll arrest you for that."

"You'll need court for that arrest," I said. "Witnesses. But nobody here wants to swear to this little scenario in open court."

I leaned down closer to Van Leer. His eyes had lost their sparkle and dulled back to how they had been.

"Mr. Van Leer, sir," I said so that nobody could hear. "We don't blame you for that temporary loss of dignity. But we do need to know if the storm has passed."

He glared at me.

"Then I stay on your feet, sir," I said.

He considered that.

"It's past," he said.

"I thought so. As I said, I feel that he will call back again. Just as you are a businessman, Mr. Van Leer, so is he. His only capitol is your daughter's safety. He will not spend that unless he has to."

Evers slapped Runyon's weightlifter back.

"It's just one piddling Neglect-of-Duty complaint, Runny," she said. "Lots of agents get them."

"Did you?" Runyon asked.

"Not yet. But if an agent never gets some kind of complaint, that agent is damn sure not doing their job."

"Some haters," Runyon said. "Some racist Klansmen types will use the N-word to describe a black agent in his neglect of duty."

"So what?" Evers said. "Some haters think that all blacks are lazy or thieves or both. Who cares?"

Chichak unsnapped his own cellphone and pressed a button.

Somber flute music came from upstairs. It sounded like Eric Satie.

"Good evening," he said into the phone. "Give me the OPR agent riding the night desk."

The agents looked at Chichak in wonder.

"Nobody calls OPR," Diascu said.

"What's 'OPR'?" I asked Diascu.

"Office of Professional Responsibility. Our Internal Affairs bunch. Nobody talks to any of them. They're like lepers."

"Something must be eating them," I said.

"Something must be eating DAD Chichak," Diascu said. "To call them, I mean."

"Hello," Chichak said into the phone. "I want to file an official complaint against a senior agent for making a racially divisive comment with civilians present," he said. "The name of the person responsible is Wilbur W. Chichak, Deputy Assistant Director. You say that you recognize my voice? Yes, that's me. I want to report myself."

"Maybe Chichak is the agent who has cracked up," Diascu said. "Nobody normal reports himself."

"Maybe the phone's not working," I said. "Just a thought."

"Because OPR does not play fair," Evers said. Her eyes pooled over her face, withdrawing into themselves.

"They have forgotten why they became agents in the first place," Diascu said.

"This talk is getting too heavy for me," Evers said.

She left us, moving past in a swirl of white lace. Levin glared at me and then left. He was probably going to gossip about this. People like Levin terrified me. They formed lynch mobs against outsiders like me.

"I respect Chichak for doing it," I said. "But I don't think that it will help the case."

"What do you care?" Diascu asked.

"I care because solving it is my only way to stay out of prison."

"That's a fantasy," Diascu said. "You think that a bloody-mouthed booze deliveryman with liquor on his breath can out-think the FBI?"

Chapter 9

THE GOVERNMENT GETS HUNGRY– 8:46 P.M.

The dining room fell quiet again.

"Go clean yourself up," the Latino agent told me. "Nobody can deal with you looking like that."

"Do it," Chichak said.

I eased myself into the wood-paneled bathroom. It had a huge porcelain sink with golden spigots shaped like fish. The wide mirror showed blood caked on my lips and neck. Dirt from somewhere smudged my hands and chin. Soap and hot water scoured me cleaner. My socks and sneaker still oozed water, but I looked fresher now.

"Much better," Chichak said when I returned.

He sighed and unfolded his cellphone and punched in a number.

"Runyon," he said, "remember that you are now liaison between Mr. Van Leer and me. That way, we avoid duplication of effort. Can you ask him what liquor store sent this delivery-man Max to him?"

Runyon nodded and left.

I turned to Chichack.

"That won't get you anything," I said. "I'm off the books. They won't admit that to the FBI and get themselves in tax-type troubles."

Chichak scrutinized me.

"Working off the books, huh?" he said. "No trace of you. No ID."

When he frisked me, his fingers had touched my wallet. I hoped that he had forgotten that.

"And look at your clothes," he went on. "Kid stuff. Leather bomber jacket, for the pilot that you were never disciplined enough to be. Cheap blue jeans, terrible shirt and wearing sneakers in the winter."

"The snowstorm took us by surprise," I said.

"And you didn't plan to walk far. That means that you live near that liquor store."

This talk was going to uncomfortable places.

"Or I could have taken the subway there," I said. "There's a subway stop on the corner."

"Corner of where?"

"Corner of where you're about to learn that the delivery came from," I said. "Tash's Liquor on 86th and Lexington."

Runyon's voice buzzed in Chichak's cellphone.

Chichak listened, nodded and hung up without saying much.

"Are you grooming Runyon for a glorious career in the Bureau?" I asked.

He shot me a look.

"What gives you that idea?" he said. "He's just one of my many agents. I try to help all of them along the way, without playing favorites."

It was time to let that one pass by.

"You called it right, Max," he said. "Tash's Liquor Store on 86th Street and Lexington. Right near the subway, as you said."

"Now, why don't you save us all this haring around, my friend?" he asked.

His voice ground down by millimeters to a confidential tone, between intimates or club members.

It was the sound of a busy important world-shaker counseling the busboy on how to get ahead in Life.

That grated on everything inside me. All the similar interviews since I was a youngster came flashing back to me.

Types like Chichak had fed me the line in school, jobs and the Department, burned me down and then moved on. I was not buying his act tonight.

"Just the last name, Max," he said. "And I guarantee you that you're going to feel a whole lot better. Make the rest of your life a whole lot easier."

"Since it's Christmastime in Manhattan," I said, "just call me Holden Caulfield."

Chichak's teeth came together. For the first time, I noticed that some of the bottom ones were crooked. That marked him as being a low-income kid who had worked his way up to here.

"My daughter once asked me to explain that book to her," he said. "I told her losers and wisecrackers always wind up in trouble that they make for themselves. Despite the catchy talk, they are not very interesting people."

He signaled to two agents standing just outside the doorway.

"Agents Wetzel and York will bring you to Tash's liquor store —"

"If they're open."

"If they're still open, as you say. We hope that they are. But we cannot conduct this type of interview by telephone. The owner must visually identify you and then give us a statement."

"Good luck with that," I said. "I do fear that you are just spinning your wheels."

"Do we have to take him now?" the smaller agent asked. "I mean, we were going real good, interviewing the guests and all, back at that townhouse."

"Wetzel, I saw you drooling in that brownstone and pretending that it was yours," Chichak said. "You, too, York. Just take this man and get him ID'd. Or would you rather be standing post outside, blocking off this street?"

"Naw, Boss," the man that he called Wetzel said. "We'll do whatever you say."

"Sure will," the other man, York, agreed.

Wetzel looked like a jumpy Airedale, with his mouth half-open as he looked me over with quick, manic eyes. A brief moustache did nothing for him. Maybe the moustache was making up for the thinning dark hair above his high forehead. A wiry build showed in the tuxedo. And the tuxedo itself had spots on the lapel and a torn pocket on the left side.

Chichak conferred with Wetzel so that I could not hear.

The agents pulled on drab raincoats that needed dry-cleaning and went outside. I did not want to be alone with them.

Wetzel motioned me inside his car. It smelled of a piney-woods car deodorizer.

York got in the front seat.

He was bulkier than Wetzel, with a broad face and another Government Service-type moustache. Moles dotted his neck and chin. His dark hair was done in a trim pompadour, old-fashioned style.

"Special Agent Bob York," he said. He gave me a hard hand to shake. Tonight everyone seemed to have a stronger grip than I did.

"Our friend here is halfway to being a subject," Wetzel said as he started the car. "Subject to our own investigation, that is."

"Well, I hope that it won't come to that," York said to me.

He acted like we shared a secret already.

"Jail and all that. Jail sucks," York intoned.

He did not know for real. He had not slept in a jail. But I had.

Wetzel guided the car out onto the streets. The snow was still lancing down.

"This sucks," York said.

He seemed to favor that expression, "sucks."

"Give me the Key West Resident Agency any day."

"And I'm starving to death," Wetzel said. "That dinner did nothing to fill me up."

"That's because you skipped lunch to have room for their dinner. You always do that before a free dinner."

"It's the principle of the thing."

"And all these richie-rich restaurants around here are either closing for the storm or gouging us on their prices," Wetzel said.

"Here's a donut shop," York said. "The Sincere Donut Shop. How expensive could they be?"

"Everything is so goddamn expensive now," Wetzel said.

They both glared at me, then continued griping about this and that as they swapped clichés.

Wetzel put the car into a bus stop at the corner of 75th Street and placed a placard laminated with a U.S. Government eagle on the dashboard. Below the bird were the words "Federal Bureau of Investigation – Official Business."

"We can't leave him in the car," York said. "Regulations."

"My name is Max, guys," I said.

"And what's your last name?" York asked.

"Aye, there's the rub," I said.

We trudged through the accumulating snow to the Sincere Donut Shop, a hole-in-the-wall that never closed.

And where the workers knew me well.

&

The shop had three small tables with chairs. On late nights, the poor and those fortunate enough to live in the Playpen but not lucky enough to share in its largess would cluster there and swap life stories over coffee growing cold. I fit right in.

"Hey, Mister Max!" Ali from Egypt greeted me from behind the counter. "Kay-fah-all?"

Or "How are you?" in Arabic.

His great luminous eyes glowed in his unshaved face.

"Anah yi-tib," I answered back. "I'm okay."

Fighting federal custody, hunger myself and the flu, it was not strictly true.

I was not okay.

"You want coffee, my friend?" Ali asked.

"You know this man?" York asked, jumping in like an amateur cop instead of letting the talk flow without having to demand.

Ali took in the tuxedos that both wore and the sleepy look of presumed authority. Third-worlders could usually sense cops. Their survival depended on it.

Ali ducked his head down.

"Know him, little bit," he said. "You gentlemen want coffee?"

"I'm still starving, Max," Wetzel said. He had enough smarts to play things as if we were all pals out on the town, enjoying the blizzard. His partner York probably drove him crazy sometimes, jumping in without thinking . "What's good here?"

"They do a great hot roast beef sandwich, with onions and gravy," I said.

"How much is it?"

"Are either of you guys married?" I asked.

"No. Neither of us," York said. "Why do you ask?"

"Because you keep grousing about the price of things. Getting married and having kids at today's prices would blow your minds. Life is expensive, guys. It takes everything that we have."

"I'll have the hot roast beef sandwich," Wetzel said.

"I'll have the same thing," York said. "Make sure that it's good and hot."

My new pals were embarrassing me in my own hangout. But I was not here as their guest.

"Of course, sir," Ali said. "And coffees for everyone, yes?"

"What language was that you spoke with him?" York asked.

This was the FBI, I reminded myself.

"That was Arabic."

"Sure it was," Wetzel said. "You remember those tapes they made us listen to?"

"Terrorist stuff," York said. "Propaganda, mostly."

"Do you speak Arabic, Max?"

"Don't start thinking 'terrorist'," I said. "Didn't you have to take a foreign language in school?"

"I damned sure didn't have to take Arabic."

Nobody else was in the shop. On a storm night like tonight, the homeless would head down to Grand Central Station and nap early. That way, when the MTA cops closed the station and pushed them outside, they were rested and refreshed from their earlier sleep.

"Let me tell you something about the prices in this town and what the FBI pays its special agents," York said. "Both Bob and I own our own homes, we walk to the subway for our transportation, and we don't hang out in clubs."

"You do," Wetzel said. "When somebody else is picking up the tab."

"You eat pizza for lunch four times a week," York said. "And you won't buy a soda. You beg a cup of tap water from the Mafia soldier running the oven."

"Every time we sit down in a real restaurant, you embarrass me. You always send one dish back. Always."

"If they don't do it right, I'm not paying for it," groused Wetzel.

"What about you? You never date anymore."

"Who needs the heartbreak? I go down to the Dominican Republic twice a year, find a playmate and everyone's happy. This free enterprise courtship will kill you."

Therapists say that being stingy can become an addiction as much as drugs or booze, I reminded myself.

"Let's stop being touchy-feely with this coffee jockey," York said. "If we can find out about Max, Chichak will be happy with us both. He could put us on a real soft detail."

"Your detail could not be any softer," Wetzel said. "Not the way you do it."

York got up and went to Ali behind the counter.

"Hey," York said, pointing at me. "Do you know this man? What's his name?"

"Sandwich coming right up, my friend."

"I asked you what his name is."

"He is good man."

"Sit down and drink your coffee," Wetzel snapped at York. "You're wasting everyone's time."

"I think that he work with you," Ali said. "Government man, yes?"

I tried not to jerk upright. Ali had no idea that I had been a cop. Very few people did. He had never seen me talk to any cop. But tonight he had seen a connection, a kinship, in the way that we sat and talked. It was if we worked for the same construction boss. And if Ali sensed that they were Government employees, then maybe I was, too.

York and Wetzel were too noisy to sense the connection.

"He calls you a Government man," Wetzel said. "Maybe we better mention that to Chichak."

My insides iced up. But I forced a phony smile.

"Do that," I said, gambling. "I'd like to see Chichak's face when you do that. Give him his only laugh of the night."

"You are really reaching on that one, pal," his partner said.

"Ali," I said. "Bathroom?"

"Right there, my friend," Ali said. He pointed to the door behind the oven.

"Don't try anything that you'll regret, Max," York said.

"Guys, it's seven feet away," I said. "And there's no window. What am I going to do? Flush myself away and wind up in the East River?"

I went inside the bathroom. Ali always kept it immaculate.

Using my ballpoint pen, I scribbled my lawyer Simon's phone number on the wall and wrote: "Tell Simon that they still have me. I need that van to clear myself. Call Murray and the other Irregulars."

Next to that, I scribbled down a description of my van, complete with license plate, bumper stickers and dents.

Then I came back outside.

"The bathroom is filthy!" I said to the agents. "You don't want to go there."

I knew that Ali would check the bathroom, see the wall and call Simon.

"Here is your sandwich, my friend," Ali said, bringing it to Wetzel. "Everything excellent good, yes?"

York looked at the sandwich and then at the menu on the wall. His wide face assumed a look of horror.

"Nine dollars for this?" York asked. "Jesus H. Christ on little rubber crutches! There's only four slices of roast beef on here."

"Sit down, for Chrissake," Wetzel said. "Chichak did not want us stopping anywhere anyway."

"Naw," York said. "This ain't right. Not at nine bucks."

He got up and brought the tray and sandwich back to Ali. Ali looked him over.

"More roast beef, here, mister," York said. "This is a little chintzy here, don't you think?"

"Excuse me extremely?" Ali asked.

"Get with it, man," York said. He dug onto his tuxedo inside pocket and came out with his credentials folder with the gold badge pinned to it. "FBI! More roast beef!"

Chapter 10

WATCH TASH DANCE– 9:30 P.M.

"Well, they'll remember us in the Sincere Donut Shop," I said inside the FBI car.

York and Wetzel fumed in silence.

Somehow, I was finding an inside hook to them.

"Why you driving so fast?" York asked Wetzel. "Snow's still coming down."

Again, the ex-cop in me enjoyed deviling the FBI.

"Maybe because Chichak is already expecting you to report back about who I am," I said. "Instead of unauthorized coffee breaks that embarrass the Bureau."

"I understood that you can be quite annoying," York said.

"Me? Naw," I said. "In fact, I know that you guys have an impossible job to do. People who go around saying that FBI stands for 'Famous But Incompetent' are all wrong, aren't they?"

"Whatever you say."

"But one of you tonight said 'Washington was the folks that brought you the World Trade Center'," I said. "What did they mean by that?"

"Some agents had information –" York began.

"Don't tell him that," Wetzel objected.

"It's been plastered in the media already," York said. "Every boat-rocker knows it."

"I'm surprised that this loudmouth boat-rocker with us tonight doesn't know the story already."

"Okay, Max," York said. "Before 9/11 went down, a female FBI agent in the Midwest heard chatter of Middle Eastern men taking flying lessons. Their English was so frickin' lousy that the jerks couldn't understand most of the lessons. No job offers from no airlines. No military backgrounds. And they did not care about lessons in how to take off or land. Money was no object."

"That would get your attention right there," Wetzel said.

"All they cared about was frickin' flying it in mid-flight. This made the frickin' agent wonder, 'I mean, is that any way to run an airline?'"

"I think that I heard something about this," I said.

"Damned betcha. This agent, Colleen Rowley, checked and applied for search warrants on these boobs. She was a lawyer as well as an agent."

"We call them "la-gents," Wetzel said.

"Everything that she frickin' needed, she had to get with a gol-danged search warrant. That was the law. Search warrant or no search is possible. Civilians, jodies, like you joke about us. But we sometimes die in a dirty alley because we follow the law.

"Then Washington said 'no deal.' Pretty much the same thing went down in Arizona, another agent named Williams with A-rabs in the skies."

"Take it light," Wetzel said.

"Those two agents alone, if Washington had backed them up, could have stopped the Trade Center bombing."

"Maybe," Wetzel said. "You can't predict a thing like that. Too many variables."

"That's why no real agent trusts Washington," York said. "Not if we want to put the bad guys where they frickin' belong."

 number

"Here we are, Tash's Liquor Store," Wetzel. "I hope you don't make things tougher on yourself, Max."

York and I slushed out into the snowfall.

"I'm surprised he's still open," York said. "Customers must want their booze to ride out the storm. Just so you don't think Wetzel is a wasted badge, he went undercover for two years and put a whole gang of pill-rolling doctors into prison. Dangerous, nasty work, with millions of fed Medicare cash at stake. And he had to pretend to be a hypochondriac."

"That was no pretending," Wetzel said, coming up behind us. "I am one. Pay doctors to count the spots on my back. And York here got his leg burned last year pulling a kid out of a car fire. Four months of therapy. Did you join the Bureau to fight fires?"

❣

We entered Tash's store. Six lanes of people and a huge display window showed that business was good.

About twenty snow-flecked customers shopped. They were New Yorkers minding their own business.

The Ethiopian cashier looked up at us. She plumed out a breathy smile. Her full breasts rose over a flat stomach and slim hips. Her teakwood-colored face showed high cheekbones under magic dark eyes. In her native language, Amharic, her first name proved impossible for Yankees like me to pronounce. So she called herself "Betty."

"Max," Betty said.

York and Wetzel ogled her.

"Do you know him?" Wetzel asked.

"Max," she said.

"Give her a pass, guys," I said. "English is not her strong suit. Her pals help her out with tough words. You want the boss, Tash."

Betty turned, unaware that she was showing them her hips and profile. Their eyes widened as they gaped. They were probably thinking of saving travel fare to the Dominican Republic to see what they could talk this one into.

"What's his last name?" Wetzel the hypochondriac asked.

Betty's eyes scrunched shut. She was trying hard to remember and be helpful.

Then she opened her eyes. With luck, I could make it out the front door, hit the street and hunt my van myself. If

Simon had called them, the Playpen Irregulars should be out searching for hours now.

These two might try to grab me if they got energetic. But they would not chase me for long in this snow. On this corner, I could run to the subway and choose six different exits to flee.

They might think about shooting me, even though it would be a bad shoot on their records. Hopefully, they knew that, too.

"What's his last name?" Wetzel reminded her helpfully.

"Max," Betty said.

"Max Max," York said. "Chichak's going to love that."

"No, no!" Wetzel said. "His last name."

Her smile was something to cherish.

"Max," she said.

"Listen up," York said, flipping open his credentials case. "We are the FBI. And we don't play games."

"Except at retirement parties," I said.

"And we want to know his last name."

"Guys, she just doesn't know," I said. "Like the Bible says, 'If you don't have the cards, then you can't deal them.'"

Customers eddied away from us. They did not like being around any of this imbroglio.

"Gentleman," Tash said from the vodka section.

He stood a crinkled six-foot-three with an odd-shaped sloping face that seemed to slouch down from his skull to his neck. Curly brown hair burst up above tortoise-shell glasses. His forehead was high enough to unbalance the rest of his face. It gave the look of the brain advancing ahead of the rest of the body.

As usual, he wore a spotless dress suit. Tonight's was a heavy brownish tweed against the weather. "I'm Tash. How may I help you?"

"This man here is a possible subject in a kidnapping case," York said. "He says that he drives a van for you. And we need his last name."

"I see," Tash said. "Why don't we step into my office for some privacy?"

He ushered us into an office with paperback editions of Zola, Dante, Cervantes and their writing pals crammed on the shelves behind him.

My thumbs twitched. Tash could react in many ways to this talk. For more than 35 years, he had been surprising me, since that morning that he had showed up at my school as a substitute teacher.

"Have you asked him his last name?" Tash said. "If he hasn't told you, then there must be a good reason for it."

"We know that," York said, showing his credentials again.

"Hold on there, just a sec, please," Tash tapped a pen against paper. "Names, please, gentlemen."

They gave them.

Tash took his time writing it down. That look on his face said that he was deciding to become a bit prickly. My feet rocked backwards off the ball and onto the heel. I cooled it. Tash was going to come through for me.

"And is this man under arrest? Can't you take his fingerprints then and get his name? I don't mean to tell you gentlemen your jobs, but that seems easier."

"Does he drive for you?"

"Yes, he does."

"Fine," Wetzel smiled. "And what's his last name?"

"Oh, come now, gentlemen, I don't recall that right now. But it may come to me later."

"There's a lot of that going around tonight," I said.

"Please check your records."

"Oh, that. He works off the books."

"You're admitting that? To us? The FBI?"

"Why not?" Tash said. "It's the truth."

Tash was turning this interview upside down to his advantage. The agents looked at the floor and then each other.

"And what about the van that he was driving?"

"Yes, that's our van."

"You let him drive your van while he is working off the books?"

"Come on, York," I said. "You going to write me a traffic ticket?"

"Half the van drivers in Manhattan drive off the books," Tash said.

"I just want you to realize that you could be arrested and prosecuted for this," Wetzel said.

Tash's high forehead crinkled some more.

"For memory loss?" Tash asked.

"For accessory after the fact to a kidnapping. And for Lying-to-a-Federal Officer."

Tash was too courtly to yawn. But he looked as if he wanted to.

"Max," he said. "I am chagrined that you have lost my van. That van was like a second home to me. Not to be indiscreet, but I admired that van more than I did my wife. One was a lot more trouble than the other. And now, you have lost it."

Tash had once told me that he had wanted to be a stand-up comedian. The FBI and I were giving him good audience tonight.

"In fact, sir," his voice rose and kept climbing, "I am APPALLED!"

His voice rocked against the walls of the office. The agents stared at him.

"That was a treasured artifact," Tash said. "It may be taken across state lines by some malefactor. I should contact the FBI."

Tash arose and paced his own stage. I believe that in his mind he was playing Falstaff in the Globe Theater.

"I do not know what you are playing at, sir," Wetzel said. "But you had best stop it now and answer our questions."

"Gentlemen, I have answered your questions to the best of my ability," Tash said. "Please ask me whatever you wish."

"Well, you've got a business and a reputation to protect here," Wetzel said. "I hope that you realize that. That cashier girl, is she a citizen?"

I slapped a foot down on the linoleum floor. It made noise. Everyone twitched.

"She is a naturalized citizen," I lied, winging it. "Under the Genocide Refugee Act, brought into the States by her sponsor,

U.S. Congresswoman Doniphan. Would your boss Chichak like a call from the Congresswoman Doniphan to clear that up?"

They shook their heads.

It was going to be a chilly ride back to Van Leer's house.

Wetzel got up and stepped closer to Tash. He thumbed at me.

"Sir, talking to you is like talking to him," Wetzel said. "Are you two related?"

"What will we find about you in our files, Mr. Tash?" York asked.

"Oh, that I've been in trouble for remembering our Constitution too clearly," Tash said. "Threatened with arrest, just like now. Beaten and jailed for protesting peacefully. But I was defended very ably and was acquitted of all charges."

"Who defended you so ably?" Wetzel asked.

Tash smiled.

"I did," he said.

"And I bet you're a lawyer, too," York said.

"No. Just an American who loves the Constitution. Ever since I got the Bronze Star in Vietnam."

"We're going to ask you a few more questions, Mr. Tash," Wetzel said.

"Except tonight," I said. "Bob, remember that doctor's appointment you have with your doctor?"

Tash picked up on it. Then he nodded his head.

"Yes, that's right," Tash said. "Gentlemen, we'll have to postpone our talk. I have a medical appointment now that I cannot miss."

"In a blizzard at this time of night?" York demanded.

"My doctor is somewhat eccentric."

"I just bet he is," Wetzel said.

"What's his name?" York asked.

I shook my head.

"Oh, gentlemen, I don't think that's germane," Tash said. "And, because of his practice, that involves some privacy issues."

"Maybe he's going to see the cock doctor," I said. "And he doesn't want the FBI to know."

Wetzel glared at me.

"No name?" York asked Tash.

"Gentlemen, I'm sorry. But –"

"Thank you for your time," Wetzel said. "We'll be in touch. Good night, sir."

☙

The agents brought me back through the store.

"Just our luck," York said. "Max here is working for a Communist red-diaper baby."

"Redder than a fire truck," Wetzel said. "But I may stop back here and take that easy-on-the-eyes cashier little gal out for a drink."

"I wouldn't," I lied. This lie was going to be fun. "Not if I were you."

"Why not?"

I rolled my eyes. Wetzel the hypochondriac gaped at me.

"You mean, diseases and stuff?" he asked. "From Africa? Oh, no!"

Chapter 11

The Lady of the House – 10:27 P.M.

Agents still blocked off the street in front of the Van Leer's.

Wetzel and York trailed me going inside the brownstone. By now, it was starting to feel like home.

"You better keep those agents there until you can search this block by daylight," I said. "There may be trace evidence that the kidnapper left behind him because the snow was just starting when this went down."

"You've got some nerve, telling us that," York said. His wide face twisted with feelings. "I never had a subject order me around so much."

"For real," Wetzel said. "Do you think that we don't know this stuff? Do you?"

We went through a group of glittery socialites in the foyer, including Santa Claus Pin, Preston and Patrician Eyeglasses, working on their drinks and talk. I wondered why they were downstairs now. Maybe they wanted to see today's FBI in action. This might become the new Playpen spectator sport, like watching the U.S. Tennis Open in Forest Hills.

"Of course, there is always some jealousy between sisters," Santa Claus Pin said. "But not like this. I mean, really."

His tone made me wonder if she was talking about Huggy's family.

"See how Playpenners are different from you agents," I said. "You and I got to parties, find a beer and a good chair and sit in it. Playpenners stand at parties. They want to show their strength and flexibility. Very few work with their bodies –"

"Very few work. Period," Wetzel said.

"– so they need to burn up the nervous energy somehow," I said. "So they stand. Often, in doorways. They clog up the doorway, talking that talk and ignoring anyone wanting to get through. Because what they have to say is So Very Important.

"That's the same reason that their parties have background music that is muted and quiet. Loud music is for working class people. Playpenners believe that their own words are music enough. Because what Playpenners have to say is vital. Their parents, nannies and private school teachers have told them so since they learned to talk. Nobody has contradicted them since they were freshmen in high school."

"You seem to have a lot to say yourself," Wetzel said to me.

"Sure. I grew up working class in the Playpen."

Chichak was giving crisp instruction to a group of notepad clutching, tuxedoed agents. He dismissed them and brought us around him.

"Before we start," Chichak said, "the Field Office got a call from some donut shop manager about some idiot impersonating an FBI agent. And not paying his bill. It is the kind of call that I would dismiss out of hand."

Searching Chichak's eyes, I looked to see if there was any hidden humor there and whether he was joking. I could not tell.

In the donut shop, we had all paid for our food. But Chichak had gotten this complaint from a manager. Ali was not a manager. So Ali must have called his manager to complain. Somebody had decided to spice up the story by saying that we had not paid. My money was on the manager.

"Do you have time right now for this kind of schoolboy nonsense?" I asked. "Don't you keep yammering that you have a life to save now?"

"The Bureau takes any alleged impersonation of its personnel very seriously."

"I'm starting to think that the Bureau takes empty candy wrappers very seriously," I said.

"We were born in frightening times when no schoolchild was safe from kidnapping."

Chichak turned professorial on me.

"Lindbergh, the first man to fly the Atlantic and an international hero, suffered his infant son kidnapped and murdered. All the police of America could do nothing. So the Bureau re-made itself from a collection of rascals, amateur detectives, hacks, do-nothings –"

"People like you, Max," York put in.

"– to combat kidnappings," Chichak went on. "Now, when some coward plans a kidnapping, we are what he worries about the most."

"I've enjoyed all the movies about you," I said. "So I already know the story."

"But tonight is not the movies, Max. We will crack this kidnapping the same way that we crack others. But we keep strict discipline along the way."

I realized that Old Chichak was a good boss. That surprised me. He was not just wasting time with this lecture. Somewhere, deep inside, he knew that Wetzel and York had triggered this complaint in the donut shop. He knew which of his agents would goof off and steal a coffee break.

By lecturing me now, he was giving them precious time to decide how to craft their stories.

"And, Max, we have an OPR, Office of Professional Responsibility, who investigate every complaint against us thoroughly. Some agents fear them and call them 'the Headhunters'. But they keep us the respected agency that we are."

"I saw that movie, too."

"Max, get your teenage wisecracking self away from us," Chichak said. "We need some privacy."

We were still standing in the foyer and the cold wind chafed at my ankles every time someone opened the front door.

This was turning into one frosty Manhattan night.

Van Leer went past from the kitchen with a slim blonde woman whose eyes showed signs of recent tears. A ring sparkled on her left hand. She would be the wife, Huggy's mother. I wondered where she had been all this time. Maybe she had been crying or tossing down antidepressants.

Van Leer left her to go upstairs. She stepped to me.

"Your face is all bruised," she said. "You must be the man that he beat up when he was taking our daughter. I'm Cornelia Van Leer."

With her thick blonde hair and blue eyes turned luminous by tears, she looked like a dignified oil painting from the Hapsburg Empire a century ago. She hinted at a past that was long gone.

Her fair skin was thickening with age; her jaw line was starting to blur. But the teary eyes focused on me, saying that she had things to say and that she would survive this night of new horrors.

She had the same wiry build that Huggy had, with thin, high shoulders and exquisite collarbones enhanced by her low-cut violet dress. Her corded arms and wrists looked as if she swung a steel tennis racket or swam laps religiously in a country-club pool.

"I'm just trying to help, Mrs. Van Leer," I said. "My name is Max."

"Has anyone looked at you for internal injuries or anything like that?"

"The FBI is giving me close attention," I said, trying to lull her into talking. "I went to Collegiate School," I lied. "And there was a boy named Van Leer there. We played soccer together."

"No boys in our branch of the family," she said. "Just Bess and Huggy. Maybe my husband's cousins."

"Collegiate was thinking of going co-ed then," I said, still lying.

"No. We were always happy with Miss Whippo's School. That's where I went, actually, a thousand years ago."

That brought my head up. This was an angle that I could work.

"Miss Whippo's on 70th Street?" I asked.

"Could there be any other? I mean, with that name."

"Mrs. Van Leer, I don't want to sound like someone out of *True Crime*. But is there anyone angry at you or your family? Could there be any personal reason for this kidnapping?"

"Are you a policeman?"

"No, I'm not." Being very careful to keep my answer in the present tense.

"What brought you here tonight? I forget, with all this hurly-burly."

"I was delivering your wine."

My answer sounded weaker as time passed.

"Oh, it was Château Pontet Canet Pauillac." Her accent was flawless. "I'd forgotten."

The shiny blue eyes blinked.

"Thank you for what you did," she said. "Or tried to do."

I was being dismissed.

Maybe I should go deliver some more giggle water and leave the adults alone.

ভ

Hoping to hear more inside baseball, I edged back to the three chums whispering.

"That question that you asked about the donut shop," Wetzel said. "I'm not sure that you really want an answer."

York's cellphone buzzed.

He scooped it up, listened and put it on speaker.

"This is Mr. Tash from this subject's liquor store," York said. "Mr. Tash, go ahead, sir."

"I called your office, and they patched me through to you," Tash's voice came through. "After you left, I checked our records on that van that Max was driving. It was long overdue for a complete tune-up. The radiator was about to fall apart. Water pump, fan belt, everything. I'd be surprised if it could go thirty miles. It's still in the city."

"You're a liquor store in a prime location," York said. "How can you let your vehicle so damn sorry?"

York's voice was changing now. It showed a slight country accent. Maybe he was remembering fixing up his first jalopy

"We've had a busy holiday season, I'm afraid," Tash said.

"Thank you, Mr. Tash," York said. "If you have any more information, please contact us."

Maybe York was sharper than I had thought, I thought. Or else the Bureau did really train their agents well.

"What's your take on this info about the van?" Chichak asked.

The agents glanced my way.

"It's okay," Chichak said. "We can speak in front of our friend Max here. I have a plan that I know will appeal to him."

That news chilled me. He might mean arresting me. My last meal was a breakfast special at the Mansion Restaurant on York Avenue about ten hours ago. By now, the dinner in jail was finished. Aside from losing this case, I would be starving and cranky all night.

Phones buzzed. All of them.

An agent's radio blurted out nearby.

"New York Base, I'm following a van resembling the kidnap vehicle," the radio said. "Now heading down York Ave and Seven-Nine Street, moving fast."

Chichak bolted. So did I. The Patrol habits made me run with him.

"That's the Crackup's voice!" York said. "I know my voices."

"That's right!" Wetzel shouted. "The same!"

"You two stay," Chichak shouted at York and Wetzel. "C-4 Squad stays, too."

Chapter 12

SNOWSLIDING – 11:01 P.M.

We all ran outside.

In a moment of weakness, Chichak had forgotten to lock the passenger door of his Caddy. I clawed it open.

Agents ran, slipped in the snow and swore, jumping into their cars.

"Where do you think that you're going?" Chichak asked. The big engine roared.

"You need me to ID the van," I panted, winded already. "That protects you from Washington."

"Like I need that."

"You all need that."

Other cars cut us off. Cream crests of snow flew from their tires.

"Goddamn baby agents," Chichak said. He used the fine-finger touch of the expert driver. He had us down the block and sluicing through ice patches before my hands could click the seat belt catch.

"New York Base, the subject van is red-balled at the intersection of East Six-Three Street and First Avenue, facing westbound. Don't know how long we got till the light changes," the radio voice said.

"What is the plate?" another radio voice asked.

"Unable to read plate with snow," the first voice said. "Vehicle now on the move, still westbound on Six-Three Street."

Chichak raced through a red light on Lexington and put the Cadillac into a skid. My body recalled other crashes. The knees came up and my head tucked down.

I tried to grope under the seat to snag my wallet. But age and stiffness were against me.

Nothing held us. We flew. It was like sliding through air. I opened my eyes.

Chichak steered into it. His face did not change expression.

Another FBI car shot past us. He just missed our front fender.

The agent inside made an "O" of shock with his mouth. Then he was swirling to our side.

Our tires caught. We steered out of the skid.

"Sweet driving," I breathed out.

Chichak did not answer. He knew what he could do.

"He's slowing down," the first voice said.

"I'm not sure that's the Crackup's voice," Chichak said.

"Don't ask him," I said. "If you ask, he might break off the surveillance."

"Your talk, Max. You must watch a slew of cop shows on daytime TV."

"He could be the Crackup and still be following my van," I said. "Even a nut can be right sometimes."

Chichak's lips quirked.

"Is that your philosophy of life, Max?"

For Chichak, that was high wit.

He brought us down Lexington to 59th Street.

"Where are they?" another radio voice said.

"Unit, your present location?"

"This is New York Base. Unit following that subject vehicle, identify yourself."

Silence followed.

"Maybe it was the Crackup," I said. "Him and J. Edgar Hoover's spirit are chasing ghosts."

"Hoover changed policing around the world and created the first agency that the perceptive, well-informed public could respect," Chichak said. "Compared to that, what have you done with your life?"

We drove on.

"Excuse me," Chichak said. "That was petty. But it irks me when civilians use his name and know nothing about him."

"That's past, Chichak. Let's work on the future."

He kept glancing at me often. I could not get my wallet now.

"All units," the first radio voice said. "Subject van is now heading east on East Five-Seven Street. Now crossing First Avenue."

"Damn!"

"Go, man, go!"

"All units," Chichak said. "Converge on the location. Any long guns nearby?"

"Roger. This is Levin with a Remington 870 shotgun, sir."

"Shotgun agent, get as close as you can," Chichak said. "Remember that we may have an innocent inside that van. All units, make sure that you have a clear shot before you trigger one. Watch your crossfire. That van could have multiple subjects inside."

"He sees me! He's running!"

"All units, this is New York Base. Subject trying to flee."

"This is operator 6041, NYPD. Do you have a pursuit within the confines of the One-Seven Precinct? Unit pursuing, please acknowledge."

Streets flew past us.

We skidded again but straightened. I smelled our engine burning.

"He's at Five-Five Street now," the unknown voice said.

Chichak wrestled the wheel and spoke into the mike.

"All units," he said. "This is DAD on the scene. I'll take the point and go in first."

"You?" I said. "You're a boss."

He hung up the radio mike.

"Bureau regs. Top rank goes first. And Bureau tradition."

"At Five-Four Street now," the unknown agent continued.

Chichak straightened out. Now I saw the van. It was flashing forward, bumping in the snow. Sirens blew.

"That might not be my van!" I said.

"Can't you tell?"

"Lighting," I said.

My head cringed. My eyes were terrible. The NYPD had ignored my eye test. I felt like the village idiot.

"Snow. Hell, I can't tell."

Cars followed the van. Their red dashboard lights bled.

More cars rocketed in. They came from every direction.

Chichak pulled ahead of them.

"This is the FBI!" a loudspeaker roared behind us. "Stop your vehicle!"

Chichak did not wait. He gunned the gas. Our front left fender bit the rear van panel. Physics worked. The van wheeled around. It lost traction.

Chichak pinned it against a parked car. Alongside us, Levin braked his own car. He jumped out and racked the pump Remington shotgun. He pointed it at the van.

Chichak threw our car in park. I jumped out. My sneakers felt the cold snow. They slipped.

The van door flew open.

Behind us, car brakes squealed. Doors slammed.

"FBI!" the loudspeaker shouted.

Chichak drew his Magnum.

The van driver showed. He jumped down from the seat and ran. His feet flew.

C&#x8;

My leg barked the door and stung me as I slopped out of the car.

I was twelve feet from the van driver. He skidded in the snow. I got closer.

"Freeze! FBI!"

He ran.

"Nobody shoot!" Chichak's voice shouted.

"Take him!" I got my legs under me and sprang.

My hands collided with his shoulders. We both went down.

"Why you running?" I shouted.

"Why you chasing me?" the van driver came back.

He smelled of rum. He kicked and caught my shin. Pain hit.

I tried to roll on top of him. He slithered away. I snagged him again. We rolled around like kids. I tried throwing a strike. It missed. Snow went down my sleeve. My skin froze. Some snow mushed into my mouth. It tasted like dirt.

Smelka and others fell onto him. One put a forearm across his skull and pressed him down in the snow. Evers elbowed him in the back, dropping down with all her body weight. Her glasses slipped off her face and into the snow.

"He's not my kidnapper!" I said. "Too big. Too old."

I repeated this twice. Somewhere behind me, I heard music playing low.

Evers speared her glasses back onto her face.

"We'll check the van," someone near me said. He smelled of coffee.

The van driver was a stout joker of fifty-something. He was balding, sported a hook nose and baggy pouches under angry snapping eyes.

The music playing behind me was a bugle cavalry charge from a Bureau car's loudspeaker. The silvery notes stretched my mouth to smile. Some agent had my sense of humor.

"This guy's so drunk that he can't hit the ground with his hat," I said. "That's why he ran."

"Is that what you do?"

"Where's the Crackup agent?" another asked. "He was following the van."

Levin's shotgun bobbed towards the van. Three agents moved behind the shotgun. One waited by the van's back door and hooked a strap to the door. Markeloy pointed his Glock at the front part.

The agent opened the door with the strap.

Levin pointed the shotgun barrel at the van.

"Van's clear!" York shouted.

"The van is empty!" Wetzel echoed.

NYPD blue-and-white cars, sirens bleating and lights spinning, roared up. Cops bellied out into the snowstorm, black jackets wetting with the snowflakes.

"You, Veds," Chichak said. "Cut off that damn cavalry charge music. You were warned before. This is not a John Ford western."

"More's the pity," Veds said, a wedge of a mustached man who strode past us.

"At least we got a drunk off the street," Diascu said.

"You non-drinking Mormon kid. Don't you know when you're outnumbered?"

"Sinful New York, sir," Diascu said. "Everyone drinks,"

I made it to the van's back bumper.

"That's not my van!" I shouted. "Chichak, the van is different."

"Are you sure?"

"Mine was a Ford. This is a Toyota."

I whacked snow off the back bumper, hurting my hand.

"And there are no dents. No bumper stickers. Different license plate."

"You're sure?"

I just looked at Chichak.

He shook his head, hugging himself in that tuxedo against the cold.

"He's drunk, so he tried to run. Human nature." Chichak said. "We'll hand him over to our locals. Listen up. Who was broadcasting this pursuit? You did a good clean job."

Nobody said anything.

Our prisoner tried kicking a cop. The cop dug in and slammed him against the patrol car and kneed him below the belt. The prisoner dropped into the snow.

Chichak tried again.

"Come on," he said. "Own up here. Sign your work."

His voice sounded hollow.

He was trying to deny something.

"It was the Crackup," Levin said. .

Chapter 13

Boys Will Be Boys – 11:28 P.M.

I returned to the Caddy and burrowed deeper in the welcome warmth.

As Chichak studied the dent created when he had edged the van, I eased my fingers into the space between the door and the seat. There was an angry thump that rattled the entire car as he slapped the damaged fender.

I touched my wallet.

Just then Chichak opened the driver's door.

Damn.

He stared at me. I pulled my hand back empty.

"I need to listen up here," Chichak said. He put his window down.

"I'll freeze," I said.

The Cadillac frame eased my back. It felt good after the chase.

""That was some skid you steered us out of," I said. "You're a better driver than I could ever be."

He looked at me.

"Long skid," he agreed.

"Longest of my life. I was afraid that we would hit the son-of-a gun sidewalk and glide right through the Bloomingdale's glass display windows. They would have found us there in the morning. Bloody and snowy, with confused looks on our mugs."

"And a smashed car to explain."

Chichak slapped me on the back. It shocked me but it felt right. It felt like being back on Patrol again. A smile stretched my face.

He shook his head, grinning. The boss was getting out of the office tonight.

"Thanks for falling on that inebriated subject," Chichak said. "You moved pretty well for a man of your size."

"I don't call it jogging anymore," I said. "I just ferry my fat around Central Park so that I can stop feeling guilty."

Through Chichack's open window we heard the other agents cat-call and guffaw. They felt the same adrenaline dump after the chase.

"Why are you still carrying a revolver with only six bullets, Wilbur?" I asked. "All your baby agents, as you call them, carry the modern semi-auto guns with sixteen rounds."

"It's a .357 Magnum Smith & Wesson. Gold-plated FBI badge on the frame. I confess to being a traditionalist."

"How?"

"Back in 1930s, gangsters were outgunning our agents. They had more money. Some converted .45 pistols to full automatic so they shot like a miniature machine gun in your hand. Our Mr. Hoover asked gunmakers for help. So Smith & Wesson designed this gun. It was the most powerful caliber in the world then. It saved the lives of many agents. Took gangsters apart and blew them to where they belonged."

"You only see pieces like that in old movies now," I said.

"An agent who was retiring gave this to me about seventeen years ago. And he had thirty-five years in the Bureau. It can still blast through anything. So there's history in this old gun."

In the high-rises flanking Lexington Avenue, Manhattanites were wrenching open windows and leaning out to peer at us in the snowstorm. Red cop lights pinked the snow that was still falling and accumulating on the ground.

Chichak pulled his tuxedo straighter and drank in the scene. Agents were folding shotguns and putting them back inside their cars.

"Smelka, didn't you hit that trashcan and scrape off some paint?" Levin asked. "Don't try covering it up. You can't hide anything from us. We are the FBI."

"I'm going to miss all this," Chichak said. "Mandatory retirement coming up soon. No more nights like tonight when everything in the world happens, and you reach back for all your training and experience to save a life."

His white head tipped upwards. He looked surprised at himself.

"With all that behind us, Max, you're still a subject in one of my cases," he said. His voice changed. "And I will have no compunction whatsoever in jailing you if necessary."

"I know."

Chapter 14

ARRESTING CONVERSATION – 11:46 P.M.

Chichak switched on the ignition and accelerated into the storm. It showed that something was chewing on him.

I tried one last time to find my wallet under the seat. It was gone. The sudden start, the chase and the skid had no doubt slid it into the Cadillac's framework. To find it now, I would probably have to take the Cadillac onto a shop and have some over-paid Playpen mechanic disembowel it.

"Maybe we better look for York and Wetzel in the kitchen, shall we?" I suggested as we climbed the steps back into the Van Leer's brownstone.

"And just why do you say that?"

"You know why, Chichak."

൬

The guests were back upstairs, roiling on a sea of Playpen party chit-chat. The liquor supply might give out. Then they would have to go outside in their tuxedos and buy Budweiser six-packs from the all-night Jonny's Freedom Market on Third Avenue.

York was holding a roast pork baguette as we entered the kitchen. He looked up as we came inside.

"Do you think the sawed-off shotgun is inside that sandwich?" I asked. "It's big enough."

"Boss."

"I know, I know," I said. "If you don't eat it, these bluebloods are going to throw it out. So you're doing them a favor. Decent of you."

His eyes bugged and rolled from strong feelings that he could not voice.

But I wanted them rattled and off-guard. If I stayed polite, their Bureau procedure would stay in place and steamroller me flat into prison.

"Where's your partner, Special Agent Wetzel?" I asked. "Testing the mattresses upstairs for clues?"

"Enough, Max," Chichak said. "We are the ones who are supposed to brutalize you. Just ask any liberal."

"Goddamn liberals like you," York said.

"Don't talk with your mouth full," I said.

"My mouth isn't full," retorted York.

"Why wait until the last minute?"

"York, can you get Wetzel down here?" Chichak asked. "I need to hear from you both what you learned from his employer."

"That won't take long," I said. "Practically nothing."

"Why don't you just shut up?" Chichak said. "Maybe permanently?"

"Catholic vow of silence?" I said. "I don't know. I tried joining the Trappist monks who live that way. But they never answer their phone."

They both gave me The Look. I was getting a lot of that tonight.

York called Wetzel on his cellphone and coaxed him into the kitchen. Nobody bothered to ask him what he had been doing. Clowns like these two had been assigned to me as partners when I was a cop. It made for long nights.

"What can you tell me about our friend Max's boss?" Chichak asked.

They told him about their encounter with Tash.

"That's it?" Chichak asked. He was crisping himself into a bad humor. I could tell. His speech sped up. He was not a street cop anymore. He was back to being a Successful-Executive-with-Confidence.

"Is this Tash character some kind of nut?" Chichak asked.

"Not to me," I said.

"I wasn't asking you," Chichak said. "York, what is your take on Tash's information?"

"I don't buy it. He did not cooperate about Max. He withheld information. He only told us what he had to, by law."

"Are you sure of that?" I asked. "Because, by law, he did not even have to say hello to you. He was not in your custody or a suspect in anything."

"Hold on," York said.

"Hold this," I said. "You run around wasting time and asking questions about me. Anyone who does not get all undressed for you, you call them a suspect."

"Max, I'll say it now," Chichak said. "Shut up."

Feeling colored his face. He was losing his cool.

"York," he went on. "Since we've got a ticking clock here, did you consider putting surveillance on that liquor store? Or on Tash? Making him a subject by virtue of his employing Max?"

York was in no hurry to answer. Party talk from upstairs sluiced down into the quiet here.

"No, I didn't," he said.

"Well, you should have. Or you, too, Wetzel. You're both experienced brick agents. It seems that this is an avenue to explore."

"My fault, boss," Wetzel said. "I just figured Tash for some loudmouth showboat."

"Well," Chichak said. "Look who he hired to do his deliveries for him. Birds of a feather, wouldn't you say?"

"Cuckoo birds," Wetzel said. He glared at me with those rolling eyes, something like a frightened horse.

This was too smooth. For my plan to work, I needed them reacting to me like the beer-pounding twenty-five-year old kids they had been. That was before they joined this Bureau and lost their freedom.

"Wetzel, and you too, York," I said, trying to churn things crazy. "It's not my fault that your boss is calling you stupid. You got that on your own."

Wetzel's nose flared. He stepped closer to me and closed his fists. I was calling him out. My plan was starting to work.

Zorah, the beauty, came inside. She looked us over and frowned when she saw me. Probably bruised, aging losers like me never spurned her body to go play detective in the snow.

For some reason, she had changed her dress and now wore a dark green gown of a muted jungle color. Women changed dresses at parties sometimes. I never understood why. It clung to her flanks. Her hair hung loosely over her bare shoulders, showing her strong, flat muscles.

All three agents watched her come in and go.

"Don't even think about trying to date her, Wetzel," I said. "You hate to spend money. You and your bachelor buddy York here. That's a Playpen beauty, pal. Lots of dinner dates, with salads and light conversation in overpriced bistros. The Playpen works by appearances, not animal appetites."

"What the hell are you talking about?" York asked.

"Walk her home. No doorstep action, either. A peck on the cheek. And even if you get her naked, you'll be disappointed in everything. She'll roll against you, half-asleep in the middle of the night and call you 'Daddy'. If you have an argument with her, she'll go put her head in the stove and turn on the gas."

"You!" Chichak said.

"Whoever spread this rumor that rich lovely women are good and happy at lovemaking was lying," I said. "He was probably trying to sell something. Perhaps it was the rich and lovely women."

"Enough side issues," Chichak breathed. "York, I hope that at least you ran this Tash for a record."

York bobbed his head and handed him a computer printout. Chichak scanned it.

"Unlawful assembly arrests," he said. "Criminal-Trespass-on-Government-Property, Assault."

"He said that he was a protestor," Wetzel said. "Some frickin' jazz about the Constitution or something."

"But no convictions," Chichak read.

"He said that he defends himself in court," Wetzel said.

"And look at the military record alongside it. Medals, citations and decorations. It's obvious that he lost his bearings, his pride of country, in Vietnam."

"Or else he regained them after Nam," I said.

"I'm putting him and his store under round-the-clock surveillance until we close this case," Chichak said.

"What a waste," I said, to disrupt him. "Chichak, instead of squandering all this time in pointless verbal interviews of the guests and Tash, you should be out doing physical work, like searching the neighborhood for my van."

Chichak stepped back in his formal black pumps. Snowmelt now crusted them. Somehow, I had wounded his vanity.

"The Bureau's fundamental core of a successful investigation is a positive and productive interview," he said. "If you were one of us, you would know that. It is drilled into every trainee at the Academy from the first day. After the interviews are completed, analyzed and double-checked, then we enter into that physical action that you keep clamoring for."

"Must be difficult to swing that when someone's shooting at you," I said.

"As we saw before, Max and this Tash boss want us searching this neighborhood for the van," Chichak said. "There may be a sinister reason for that. They may want us to forget about looking elsewhere."

"Aw, Jesus wept," I said. "Why don't you stop giving scoutmaster lectures and start working like a detective? You're playing it safe, and Huggy may die as a result."

His face flamed again.

"That's the last insult," Chichak said. "Why don't you gentlemen take Max down to the Field Office, identify him and take a statement?"

They both nodded and smirked. The rebel was being punished and the teenager grounded.

I put my chin down, boxer-style, and looked up at him. Trainers called it "sighting through your own eyebrows."

"Keep it in your pants, Mister Deputy Assistant Director," I said, growling. "I am not going voluntarily. If you want me to go, you have to arrest me right here and now."

Chichak reached under his tuxedo and brought out a pair of blued-steel handcuffs.

"But," I said. "If that happens, I get certain rights. Like a lawyer right away. That will not help your case move forward."

"I'll take that chance. Seeing you in a cell would give me great satisfaction."

My neck started sweating. It was not the flu doing it. Jail terrified me. It always did.

"And you lose another lead," I said.

"What damn lead?"

"Ms. Van Leer said that Huggy goes to Miss Whippo's School for Young Ladies. Well, I know Miss Whippo by sight. She's eighty-eight years old now and semi-retired. But she knows gossip and news about all her 158 girl students. And I happen to know where she lives, at a friend's house. She is very private. You could never get this info any way else. It just ain't on paper. At least, not tonight. So you need me."

"Like the plague," Chichak said.

"Miss Whippo knows me, too," I said. "Bring me to this talk, and I'll point out her house. You'll get stuff about Huggy that you would never get any other way."

Chichak scanned me. Then he slid the handcuffs back under the tuxedo.

"You two take him –"

"Not these two," I said. "Just like you, they would sing at my wake. You've all got your nuts twisted against me. Miss Whippo is very acute. She would mistrust them on sight. The interview would fail."

"Quite the salesman now."

I had to use his words against him now.

"You said it yourself," I said. "'The productive interview is key to a good Bureau case with nobody harmed.' If you truly believe that, send different agents with me. And if you're committed, you will send a smart woman agent. Miss Whippo will relate to her better."

"Again, I've got a subject telling me how to run my case," he said. "This reminds me of certain nightmares I had when I was a baby agent."

Chichak took out his phone again. He punched in a number.

"Hello?" a woman's voice said on the speaker.

"Gancy, this is Chichak. Have you and your partner meet me in the kitchen ASAP. I'm sending you out into the field."

"We're in the middle of interviewing a neighbor now, sir," Gancy replied. "And we just started this side of the street."

"This takes priority," Chichak said, making a hard face at me. "Five minutes, please."

A ragged cheer broke out among the guests. Somewhere, an expensive antique clock chimed midnight.

Christmas Eve had officially begun.

Chapter 15

GOING TO MEET MISS WHIPPO –
CHRISTMAS EVE, 12:07 A.M.

Special Agent Gancy was a model-thin young woman, with a sculpted face framed by stylish black hair. She moved through the foyer and then unhooked a slim ankle to step in my way. Her face snapped up to stare into mine above her. A jade amulet hung against her throat.

"DAD Chichak says for us to ferry you somewhere," she said.

"That's right," I said. "Let me explain myself to you."

"Don't bother," she said. "I saw you knock down that fat drunk van driver."

"You've come to praise me?"

"Chichak told us all about you. My G-car is near the corner. I just got here before that chase. A lot of wasted time," she said, then added somewhat redundantly "I don't like wasting time."

She moved her foot again, a shoe trimmed in elegant silver.

"I thought that you just got here recently," I said. "Otherwise, I would have noticed you in your wonderful dress."

"Ha!" she said.

Her dress was a Burgundy color, about the same shade as the carpet in Chichak's Cadillac. It swooped and clung around her frame.

"It looks like an original," I said.

"No more wasted time," she said. Her words flew faster. "Let's go right now, get it done and get back."

"I'll drive," an older man said, coming into the foyer. A New York accent grounded him nearby. He was shorter than Gancy but just as slim. Maybe FBI agents did not know how to fatten up like the rest of us.

He looked mild and scholarly, with a pale face topped by prematurely white hair.

From books, I knew that agents had to run grueling courses in the rain and mud, roll in it and come up firing their weapons accurately. They had to box each other in their Academy and go all-out. Pull-ups, push-ups and sit-ups followed until they washed in their own sweat. It seemed hard to imagine that he had gone through all that.

"You're coming?" he said, stating a fact.

"I'm sorry. My name is Max."

"They told us everything. You don't mind sitting in the back seat?"

"Not when it is suggested by the FBI."

"Right," he said. "I'm just Ray Fox to my neighbors."

I zipped up my bomber jacket, Fox slid into a heavy tweed, while Gancy buttoned up a camel's hair topcoat.

We headed out into the swirling snowstorm.

છ

"Please take me over to East 95th Street and Third Avenue," I said once we were settled in Fox's tan Chrysler New Yorker. "I don't know the address but I know the building."

"How so?" Gancy said.

"Miss Whippo is eighty-eight-years old, started her own school about fifty years ago and is not a woman that you forget. I've seen her lugging her own shopping home here. Everyone in this neighborhood, this Playpen, knows her by sight."

Gancy snorted. It sounded very delicate coming from her.

"Why do you call it 'the Playpen'?" she asked.

By the time I had finished explaining my Playpen theory, we were on East 95th Street.

"After dark, this streets looks a bit at risk for an elderly female on her own," Fox said.

"Right you are," I said. "Spanish Harlem starts two minutes uptown of here. And Spanish Harlem has always suffered from high crime. This is the boundary line."

Snow was still falling.

Miss Whippo's brownstone stood like a castle where the king had died without paying the electric bill. Architecture was never my turf, but this place looked rickety. It rose up narrow and constrained between two modern high rises. It was also the only building on the street without Christmas decorations.

"This is it here," I said. "Number 263."

Gancy took out a throat mike from her purse and spoke into it.

"New York Base," she said. "This is 7812, New York C-9. Show us out with a witness at 263 East 95th Street until further."

"Roger, 7812," a woman answered from the base radio.

Gancy's and Fox's right hands went to their right hips.

"Hey, ease up," I said. "We're just going to interview a private school headmistress."

"They trained us to be ready," Gancy said.

"You two really think alike," I said.

"We should," Fox smiled. "We are roommates. But she's about to marry another Special Agent and leave me paying the rent."

"Then she should feel peaceful and loving," I said.

"In a kidnap with violence case," Gancy said. "For all we know, the kidnapper is inside there with her."

"That's a neat trick," I said. "I can't think how that could happen."

"Everyone says that you think that you're a riot," Gancy said.

The snowfall was slowing now.

An Asian man shoveled snow across the street from Miss Whippo's brownstone, pitching full loads onto the street. A young woman in a light blue snowsuit shoveled alongside him.

Fox rang the single doorbell at 263. We listened. Nothing happened.

Gancy stepped back and looked up at the brownstone. As I said, it looked pretty grim.

Fox rang the bell again.

The snowstorm had cut traffic. New Yorkers stayed under the covers and away from their ignition keys. So the city now breathed quiet moments where I could hear anything that happened.

Nothing was.

Fox took out a business card and started to scribble on it.

"Hold that card," I said. "This lead could turn important."

He stopped writing and turned to face me.

"Would you like us to concentrate our efforts back at the kidnap scene?" he asked. His voice stayed neutral. "What do you say about checking a city block for possible witnesses?"

"Later," I said. "We are here right now."

Gancy lifted her foot a few inches and stamped it. It looked like the kind of thing that she did whenever things frustrated her. Right now, I was one of those things.

She looked up to see if I had noticed the foot-stamp.

"You folks specialize in pure energy that gets you nothing," I said. "Don't walk away from a lead just because nobody breaks their leg running to answer your ring. Now watch me use common sense and show off a bit to the FBI."

To prove my point, I slogged through the snow to where the Asian father and his daughter were churning it up. Gancy and Fox followed with dubious expressions.

"Excuse me," I tried saying over the wind. "I'm looking for Miss Whippo."

He stared at me, a spare but strong-looking man in his 70s, wearing a New York Mets baseball cap. He muttered something.

I repeated my riff.

He mumbled something back.

"Ms. Gancy, it sounds like Cantonese," I said. "Okay, here goes my baby-talk Cantonese."

I turned to the snow-shoveler.

"Ah-mah Whippo, kuy high bind-do yee-gaw?"

"Yup," Fox said. "You're showing off, all right."

The daughter stopped shoveling. She was a beauty with a cherub's face.

"Excuse me," she said in perfect English. "Are you trying to speak Cantonese?"

"Sometimes."

"I'll get Miss Whippo for you."

"You speak English," I said, like a fool.

"Of course. I go to Baruch."

Fox laughed.

"They use English all the time at Baruch University," he said to me. "Where in the world did you learn Cantonese?"

"I have a past," I said.

"If you don't start making Chichak happy, you won't have a future."

"I can just barely get understood in Cantonese," I said. "Most Chinese just laugh at me."

"Don't most people?" Gancy said.

The daughter hesitated. "It's after midnight now."

"I'm afraid that this can't wait until morning," Fox said.

"Miss Whippo goes to bed early," the daughter said.

"This is urgent," Fox droned. "Somebody's safety is at stake. My name is Fox, and I'm with the FBI."

He said it simply, with power behind it, ready to use it if needed.

The daughter crossed the street and went up to the doorbell that we had rung. She rang a code of three rings and then one ring. It might be worth remembering that later. Between the flu, my pains and pants still wet from snow, I fought to memorize it.

A ring answered hers.

We waited.

The door lock clicked.

"You can go in now," the daughter said. "Miss Whippo will meet you."

ଔ

We went through the doorway and into darkness. This was a Playpen brownstone, chopped up into apartments. A warm meaty smell filled the four stories. My body eased after the cold outside.

The agents kept their right hands in their pockets.

"This is darker than Ebenezer Scrooge's apartment," I said. "Maybe for the same reason."

"Meaning what?"

"Economy."

Snow clumped off our shoes and onto the creaky steps.

We kept climbing.

"Lee won't let anyone see me unless it's important," a woman's clear voice said above us.

That made me jump. My heart jumped into my gullet.

The agents were too well trained to shoot her.

My eyes could not penetrate the darkness above me.

"Whenever it snows, her father wants to clean up all of Manhattan with his shovel," she said. "There is no talking to him."

"Could we turn on some light, please?" I asked.

"Of course," the woman said.

All the low-wattage bulbs came on, like a thousand flickering torches in a cave. It made me blink. Standing at the open door on the landing above us, Miss Whippo stood with snapping bright blue eyes and a head of hair colored whitish gold. Her skin looked like the palest leather, with networks of laugh lines. Her face was aging, but the eyes still burned after all the years. She put a pale hand on the doorframe to steady herself.

Her burgundy bathrobe covered light pink pajamas.

"Do I know you?" she asked.

"We know each other very slightly, Miss Whippo," I said. "When you were injured –"

"Hey, Max, I got this," Gancy said.

She turned to Miss Whippo.

"Miss Whippo, the two of us here are with the FBI. He is not. We apologize for bothering you on Christmas Eve at this time of night. I'm Special Agent Elizabeth Gancy and this is Special Agent Raymond Fox."

Both displayed their credentials folders.

"May we come inside and speak with you?" Gancy said. "This gentleman can wait in the hallway, if you prefer, so that we talk privately."

"This gentleman doesn't prefer it," I said. "I'm sitting in on this one."

Gancy looked unsure for a change.

"Or else, I can still pull the plug on this interview," I said. Fox saw that I meant it.

"We are happy to have you with us," he said. "We can be flexible this once."

❧

Miss Whippo brought us inside a small living room, overstuffed with furniture in the best Victorian style. A Moroccan leather camel saddle with an ivory pommel lay atop a cabinet. Different Tibetan face masks colored the skyblue walls. Choked bookshelves ran below the masks. A fat globe, the color of aged parchment, perched on a metal rack that came up to my hip. In bookcases, cabinets and random stacks on various flat surfaces were books – all hardbacks and most with dust jackets.

The apartment smelled even more strongly of something meaty, freshly cooked. The smell teased my memory but I could not place it.

"Miss Whippo," Fox began, "our Bureau has an interest in the family of Cyrus Van Leer. Let me add that we are here with his full knowledge and cooperation."

"For what reason?" Miss Whippo asked.

She was composing herself, tightening the robe around her as Fox pulled out a notepad and pen from his raincoat.

"We're not at liberty to say right now," Gancy replied.

"What federal linoleum!" I said. "Those words mean nothing. They just cover up real talk. No wonder normal bipeds do not wish to speak with you."

"The DAD wants this incident kept quiet," Fox said.

"Goody for your Daddy," I said. "I don't work for him."

I leaned toward Miss Whippo.

– 99 –

"Ma'am, my name is Max. You and I have met a few times at functions. Back in high school, I used to date Dia Warrell. From your school."

"And then she married Brewster Barclay?" Miss Whippo asked.

"Probably. When I last saw her, she seemed to be engaged to practically everyone."

"Is that so?"

"I was living as a scholarship teenager," I said. "I could not afford dating in a discotheque. I had to hope for sunny days and coax the girls into walking Central Park with me."

"And did that work?"

"Sometimes New York has too much rain for romance," I said.

"And you went where to school?" she asked.

I shrugged. Her dredging up my past and tipping off the agents would land me in jail, just like Chichak wanted.

"Right now, I'm just helping the Van Leer family out," I said. "Their daughter Huggy was kidnapped tonight."

She did not jump up or faint. Her eyes burned a bit brighter, and she leaned closer in her cane chair.

"You two know each other?" Gancy asked.

Fox jotted down a few lines.

"Manhattan's private school world is quite exquisitely small," she said.

"Expensively small," I said. "Too pricey for the hoi polloi."

"Most of us know each other by name or reputation," Miss Whippo said. "We school and vacation together and marry each other. Few of us ever leave this neighborhood, except to retire to West Palm Beach or Southampton. Remember that I've schooled generations of girls here. So this gentleman dated someone that I taught about 30 years ago. As one ages, it all comes together."

"Miss Whippo," Gancy said. "We would prefer that you not mention this to anyone. It may hamper our efforts to get this victim back safely."

"Of course, my dear."

"What can you tell us about the family background?" Fox asked.

He spoke slowly while scribbling quickly.

"Cyrus, the father, works in petroleum and has since college," Miss Whippo answered. "Stanford University was his alma mater. He seems to be quite comfortable, from what I can gather."

"Do you know which petroleum company?" Gancy asked.

"No, I'm afraid not."

"Miss Whippo, some petroleum companies get bad press when there is any scandal about spillage, let us say. This stirs up radical elements. Has any of that happened with Mr. Van Leer?"

The agents went on like this for a while. They took turns with their questions. I just listened. They were much smoother than the NYPD detectives I'd seen conducting interviews before. But they took a while to reach their point.

Miss Whippo seemed at ease swimming through their sea of words. She had learned to suffer through parent-teacher meetings.

"And," she was saying, "just because most of my girls are born into affluent families, it does not mean that they lead happy lives."

"No?" Gancy asked. "This is one of the wealthiest neighborhoods in the world. How do your girls feel unhappy?"

"Oh, Special Agent Gancy, having money in back of you means just that," Miss Whippo said. "It does not mean that your parents were ready to have children. Your family could spend and live well, true. But what happens if your father loses his job and cannot find another?"

"That happens all the time now," Fox said.

"No matter what we do now, in today's economy, we will always have less security than our parents did. And these parents work in the corporate world, without government pensions such as you agents enjoy."

"Still, money helps everything," Gancy said. "I was an accountant before joining the Bureau."

"I also hear stories of children plotting against their parents, to get their money," Miss Whippo said. "Most of my students have done nothing except take classes and learn tennis or sailing. Even after college, they do not have the skills to survive in the outside world."

By now, I realized what the meaty cooking smell was – grilled hot dogs. That smell went back to my own childhood. Miss Whippo did not seem like a rah-rah party gal with three hot dogs and a pitcher of suds to wash them down. But maybe she was. Perhaps she needed to chomp on a couple of franks before she could hit the rack.

"Money limits one," she went on. "It often means that you grew up around those who always had it. That makes it difficult to break out into the other world. The rest of the world envies, dislikes, mistrusts and does not understand you. I don't care to re-hash F. Scott Fitzgerald, but he still remains this neighborhood's favorite and constant writer, seventy years after his death. Because the issues of wealth and privilege still haunt us here."

"How was Huggy handling her own affluence?" I asked.

"Huggy is the kind of person that does not notice much outside her sphere," Miss Whippo said. "She excites jealousy without even knowing why. Even in third grade, other girls looked at her paper to cheat. Some admitted it. Her sister did not. Others do not always understand her. There's more to life than knowing your colors."

"Excuse me, Miss Whippo," Gancy broke in. "You should know that most kidnappers just want money."

"Hold up," I said. "We don't know why this kidnapper took Huggy. Miss Whippo, what did you mean by your comment about 'colors'?"

"I didn't say anything about colors," she said.

"Excuse me but you did," I said. "You were talking about Huggy exciting jealousy in some people and you said, 'There's more to life than knowing your colors.' If you please, that excited my curiosity."

"Well, I didn't say it."

"Let's get back on solid ground," Gancy said.

"Now, wait a minute," Fox said. "I heard the comment about colors, too. It must have meant something."

Gancy made pop eyes at her partner. That was to remind her that Miss Whippo was eighty-eight-years old and maybe confused.

"There is a lot of pressure on our girls from the time they can walk," Miss Whippo said. "Sometimes their parents want too much too soon for them. I have to counsel the parents more than their children. Life is not a race to the CEO's armchair. We are here to enjoy it."

"Miss Whippo, did the family ever receive any threats?" Gancy asked.

"Oh, no. I would have told Cummings straight away."

"Who is Cummings?"

"Our Director of Security. He used to be a policeman, like you two."

"A private girl's school has a Director of Security?" Fox asked.

"We have the children and relatives of the deposed first families of Iran, Nicaragua, Afghanistan and a few others that escape my memory. There are still enough angry radicals with causes roaming around loosely. Need I remind the FBI about terrorism?"

"Not when you put it that way."

"We have a duty to protect all our students," she said. "This school has been named for me these last thirty-seven years, but I certainly do not own it. I administer it. I actually own very little."

"You and me both," I said.

"And I bring all the girls here so they see that for themselves. That a school can be named for you and run by a board of parents and teachers, but you yourself have nothing but an adequate wardrobe and too many books."

"Thank you very much for your time," Fox said.

He slid his notepad and pen back into his raincoat pocket.

We said our goodbyes and clumped down the stairs.

"Why did she forget what she said?" Gancy asked. "Is she senile?"

"Older people may get confused more easily after dark," Fox said. "It's called 'sundowning'. Doesn't mean she is senile. Just that she is older than us."

Ë

They closed their coats as we went outside.

Snow was still coming down.

The Asian father and his daughter flung snowballs at each other. They laughed and whooped over the cleared paths that they had dug.

"Let me go speak to her for a second," I said.

"Why?"

"Experience," I said, under my breath.

My feet wetted from the snow. I slogged over to the snow fighters.

They quieted when they saw me. Like many Asians, they did not show emotions easily before strangers.

Reaching back for my standard cop line, I smiled and tried to look harmless.

"Is there anything more that you want to tell me?" I asked.

"No, sir."

"Let's go!" Gancy shouted from the car.

"But a man came to see her," she said.

"To see who?"

"Miss Whippo, I think. Because she is the only one in that house now. The others are on vacation in Florida."

I stopped.

"Who came here?" I asked her.

"A man in a big car. He stopped in front of her home. Then he drove away."

"What color was this car?" I asked.

"I couldn't see because of the snow."

"You called it a big car. Was it the kind of big car that they use to carry things for work in?"

"A van, yes. What am I saying? Not a big car. A van."

"Jackpot!" I shouted through the snow at the agents as they opened the car doors. "We just got a hit!"

Chapter 16

THE SUBJECT ESCAPES – 12:45 A.M.

Fox and Gancy closed the car doors and made their way through the snow to me.

"What is it now?" Gancy asked, blowing hair from her mouth.

I told them.

"That doesn't mean that the subject came here."

They were locking their heels.

"It was a van," I said. "He came here, right, and parked in front of Miss Whippo's."

"Why would he come here?"

"Miss Whippo said that all her girls know where she lives because she invites them here. So Huggy knows this house. The kidnapper knows that we will have her family staked out. If the kidnapper wants someone to drop off ransom money, they might choose Whippo."

"That old woman? Why?"

"Because she won't fight the suspect or shoot him. She'll do as she is told. If you agents want to have a cop impersonate Whippo on the drop, you won't find any cop her age. Try finding a makeup artist tonight."

"You're reaching," Fox said.

"Am I? How good is she as a witness in court? Her eyesight may not be great. We've seen her memory fail tonight.

What if she dies before trial? Juries like to hear a live witness. They want to hear cross-examination. A dead one weakens the case, no matter how many depositions were written. And the defense jackals will use her death to their advantage."

The wind picked up and cut all of us.

The Asian woman, whom Whippo called "Lee," was still snowballing against her dad, both giggling.

"So, what if the subject did come here?" Gancy said. "What do we do with that info?"

"This may be hard for the Government to hear," I said. "But keep an open mind."

"Very funny."

"Don't look up," I said. "Just keep normal. We've got a man standing on the corner of Second Avenue. He could be watching us."

"Or watching anything else in the world," snapped Gancy.

"I don't see him," Fox said.

"He's there, anyway," I said.

The man was about eighty feet away, half-hidden in the shadows of a steel-and-glass high rise. He had not moved since I saw him. In the Playpen, that kind of stillness was rare. Nobody stood still. They were too important.

My legs shook. I could see the snowflakes hit them in between shivers. I did not want this mutt sliding away free.

"I don't think that he's involved," Gancy said.

"Do you want me to ask?" I said.

"This is all a wild-goose chase," Fox said.

"Some civilians live on a diet of wild goose," I said. "Very low-fat. It means using your imagination. You handmaidens of Uncle Sam should try it sometime."

"I see him now," Fox said. "For Chrissakes, he's going up on that stoop of that house. He probably lives there."

Now the man was standing on the doorway step of another brownstone. He swayed a bit, watching the snowstorm or us.

"Case closed," Gancy said. "Let's get back to work."

"Case wide open," I said. "I happen to know that that house where he's standing is being renovated now. Nobody lives there. He is just trying to make you think that it's his home. An old burglar's trick."

"And I bet you know a lot of them."

"How come you know that home's being fixed up?" Fox asked. "Maybe you live on this block? Or maybe you're just lying to us. I need to know more about you, pal."

"Not now. Concentrate on him."

"Of all the places in Manhattan, you know this one?" Gancy asked.

"I walk a lot," I said. "Because I got no cash. And I pay attention."

"He's not going anywhere."

My legs stayed still, for now. I would have to steel myself somewhat.

"Play it smart," I said. "Use that radio with the throat mike in your tux. Get some backup here and cover him. Then pick him up and see who he is."

"Who do you think that he is?" Fox asked.

"Our suspect. Or one of his pals."

"Come on."

"You were the ones with your hands on your guns just now," I said. "You said that you were ready for anything. Well, this is your anything."

"The subject smacked you," Gancy said. "Is this the same man?"

I squinted. My eyes were letting me down again. This was no time to explain my problems. I heaved a big sigh.

"At this distance and this light, I can't say."

"You're a real waste of time, you know that?" Gancy said. Her words sped up. She had no time for types like me.

"I don't want to hit the panic button on some drunk who likes to watch blizzards," Fox said. "Getting everyone involved."

"They're already involved," I said. "It's a major case. Work it right."

"You're a deliveryman," Gancy said. "And a subject yourself. Who are you to order us around like you're some kind of cop?"

"While we're goddamn jaw-jacking, he could go right to Hell and gone now," Fox said.

His voice climbed from tension. He did not sound scholarly anymore.

"You two stay here. I'll go around the block and come up on him from the avenue. We'll box him in and then have him good. We'll see who and what he is."

"Splitting up is not safe," I said.

"You're still a deliveryman," he snapped. "Give me about five lousy minutes."

He shouldered his way into the storm. Gancy looked down towards the man on the stoop. That was a mistake. I could see his body tighten, even at this distance. Now he knew that we were watching him. The game was going to turn wild card.

Partners always supported each other in front of outsiders. I was the complete outsider. But I had to try.

"Agent Gancy, you've got your own radio. Protect your partner. Get some agents here to seal off the block."

She just looked at me.

"I can't do that," she said. "We made a plan."

"If that joker over there has his sawed-off with him, your plan is going to change and get little noisy."

She made an ugly face and turned to look at our guy. It made me wonder what kind of work she did in the Bureau. Some agents just listened to wiretaps for years. Others checked Government job applicants.

"Let's get a little closer," she said. "It's about time."

This was getting worse.

Fox came around the corner. Our suspect saw the deal in front of him. He moved off the porch. Fox got closer.

The suspect's legs pumped. He was running now, across the street. Fox jogged to cut him off.

I was already running towards him. My sneakers slipped.

Fox was on front of him now.

"Freeze!" Fox shouted. "FBI!"

The man kept coming.

Fox drew his Glock.

"Get on the ground!"

I could see the man in the light now. He was in his thirties and the same size as the kidnapper. He could be the same man. He could also be anyone else.

The man did not stop.

He was not getting on any ground.

If that were me, I would keep going, too. Gambling everything, I lunged, hoping for a flying tackle like before. He was too quick. I flying-tackled about four feet of snowdrift. All I saw were his legs pumping up snow from the street.

Gancy was running past me now. She was clawing in her gun pocket.

The man hit Second Avenue, turned the corner and was gone.

Gancy had the radio mike up to her mouth then shook her head and put it away.

"Smart move," I said. "You'll never nail him."

"Are you going to keep lying there in the snow?"

"I was hoping that you would help me up."

She snorted again.

The Chinese father and his daughter ran over to me, holding their shovels.

"Are you hurt?" the daughter from Baruch asked. Streetlight showed her worried eyes and half-opened mouth.

"No, I'm Max. I don't know anyone named 'Hurt.' What's your name?"

"Lee."

"That's a pretty name. Reminds me of the Confederate general."

She came nearer. Up close, she looked younger than I had first thought. She reached down and flipped me over with ease. I could feel the strength in her hands as she sat me up in the snow and dusted me off. Just like her daddy, she was slim and strong.

"Oh," she said. "You look like a wet puppy playing in the snow. You'll catch cold. How do you speak Cantonese?"

"Miss," Gancy said. "Please get away from him."

"Good advice," Fox said, coming up. His gun was back under his tuxedo by now. "Permanently, if possible. He's poison to a sweet girl like you."

"Is he your prisoner?" the daughter Lee asked.

"Well, sort of," Gancy said.

Lee dropped her hands and stepped from me. Her father made a judgmental kind of look and pulled her down the block. He understood the tone, if not the words. I flopped back down in the snow. Some of the snow went from my belt-line to my spine. It hit the nerves there like an ice shower. So did Gancy's words.

"More federal linoleum!" I said. "How can I be 'kind of' a prisoner? That's like being kind of pregnant or kind of dead. You're killing my reputation in the Playpen."

"Your what?" Gancy asked.

"Let's knock it off and work," I said. "Call Chichak and tell him to stake out Whippo's address here. We may get lucky and have a return showing."

They looked at each other and then at me. To get my dignity back, I rocked to my feet. Then I read their looks at each other.

"You're not going to tell him," I said. "Well, damn my eyes. You're going to forget this little street drama because you farkled it up by not getting backup."

"Well, we don't know that he is the subject," Gancy said.

"And we don't know that he ain't," I said. "I will never get over the kids-summer-camp routine that still plagues modern policing."

"What kind of stupid talk is that?"

"It means that he is a possible suspect in this case. And you challenged him, identified yourself, drew your gun on him, and now you want to sweep it under the rug. To avoid criticism."

They looked at me from inside their child-state.

"I'll deliver you from temptation, Special Agents," I said. "If you don't tell Chichak, then I will."

"We can jail you," Fox said. "Then you won't be telling anyone anything."

"Ah, the old reliable," I said. "When everything else fails, jug them. Use your noggin, Fox. If you arrest me, I get a phone call to my lawyer. And I'll peach on you through him with a report chockfull of lovely details to your bosses."

"We were just testing you," Gancy said.

"How nice that I passed," I said.

Gancy did not like lying. It scored her face.

"You've learned how to cover yourself," I said. "Once my bosses betrayed me, I had to learn the same tap-dance steps as you."

"That's the kind of thing a cop would say," she said.

That was too close.

"I knew a lot of cops," I said truthfully. "But my eyes are terrible. I may be legally blind, so I can't be a cop. That makes me just a good listener in cop bars."

Lee and her father were slushing through the snow to their cleaner world.

"Don't let those two get away," I said. "Tell Chichak to get a sketch artist up to the brownstone ASAP. Before their memories fade. They can give you a visual description of the suspect."

"I keep telling you, you don't order us around!" Gancy said.

"Nope. I sure don't. But Washington does. So does common sense. If Huggy wakes up very dead tomorrow, and you let two possible witnesses disappear, what will those Daddy Warbucks socialites at the party do to your careers? What will Van Leer do through his worldshaker squash buddies? They'll make you both the scapegoats for the dead victim."

"Miss Lee!" Gancy said, raising her voice above the wind. "May I speak with you, please?"

Lee and her daddy heard the authority and stopped in their snowy tracks.

Gancy moved closer to settle them down and ease their minds with false promises of speedy and polite treatment at the hands of Uncle Sugar.

"The old man's no good," Fox said. "He doesn't even speak English, and he didn't get a good look at the van man."

"Are you sure?" I asked. "Look how protective he is of his daughter now. And he knows you are law. A van pulls up at night, and a man is driving it, and the van is big enough to kidnap his daughter with ease. Do you think that he's not going to look hard and concentrate on that driver's face to protect his daughter? So make sure that your sketch artist has a Cantonese interpreter with him."

"You sure got a big mouth. Do you tell the other deliverymen how to do their jobs?" Fox asked. His face and voice hardened as he tried to control himself.

"If they're about to run down innocents, yes, I do," I said. "And what kind of challenge is that, what you said to the suspect? 'Freeze! FBI!' I'm not sure that everyone understands the word 'freeze.' And is that a legal order? 'Freeze?'"

Fox looked away at Gancy making nice with Lee and Daddy of Lee.

"It's what they train us to say at the Academy," he said. "That's the standard challenge. 'Freeze. FBI.'"

"Like a lot of things in your outfit, it is too insular," I said. "You agents work like fiends, and you do great work, but the world is bigger than just the FBI. So you complicate things too much. Try saying 'FBI. Don't move.' You'll find that works better. People will obey you more. You won't have to fight so much."

Fox did not take my lecture well. His face pouted. But he knew enough to shut up until he covered himself with Chichak about drawing his piece on our unknown. He stepped away from me so he could conspire on his phone with Chichak.

Lee glanced at me and then looked away.

"I'll need your father's full name," Gancy said.

"His name is Beau Po. In English, you spell it B-E-A-U."

"We need his real name. Not a nickname."

Lee's face scrunched up trying to explain.

"But that is his real name."

"'Beau?'" Gancy said. "Do you know what that means?"

"'Pretty man' in French," Lee said. "Like Beau Brummel. When he was younger, he was very handsome, and the women made a fuss over him."

"Beau Po," Gancy said, scribbling. "Chichak's going to love that. And you?"

"I am Lee Po. They named me for the poet."

"A poet? Is he a Communist, this poet?"

"I doubt it, Special Agent," I said. "He has been just oh-so-very graveyard dead for hundreds of years."

Fox stopped mutter-plotting with Chichak and handed the phone to me.

"The last thing I want to hear from you are any new ideas," Chichak said.

"Then you better toss the phone," I said. "Because your subject may have been here. Your people do great work. Do some now. Stake out Whippo's crib."

"That van driver could have been some driver who got lost."

"It's been snowing since four-thirty. Who decides to take their van out for a pleasure spin in a blizzard? I don't. Neither do you. Then he stops in front of her place. Why? No other cars have stopped here tonight. There's a connection between him and Whippo. That connection must be Huggy."

"And why did he leave?" Chichak asked.

"Because your agents always put a parking plaque marked 'FBI' on their dashboard. I bet that they did it to-night at Whippo's. I don't remember. You ask them. They won't want to answer me. The kidnapper drives up, stops in front of Whippo's, looks around and sees the FBI plaque. So he takes off."

"Then why did he come back?"

"I don't know," I said. "Yet. But I will."

"You're twisting facts to fit your theory."

"Then twist this," I said. "Your man drew and challenged an unknown here. It could have been the suspect. Or it could have been the local Assemblyman with insomnia and laryngitis."

"So he could not answer Fox's challenge?" Chichak asked.

"Absolutely. He could be home right now, terrified of the FBI coming to exterminate him with a death squad. So he's writing a letter of complaint about your FBI to *The New York Times*, *The Village Voice*, *The Daily Worker* and anyone else who will read it. For you to protect Fox from Washington, you better treat this site at Whippo's as a new lead in the case. And you'll have to stake it out, since it is a lead. Or else, there was no lead here, Fox drew on an innocent taxpayer and he'll get five days suspension. No matter what you say, your agents will mistrust you more because it happened when you were the boss."

"I'll stake it out," Chichak said. "But that's a decision that I make. Not you. The way you talk, I wonder how you ever lasted this long without someone beating you into silence."

Chapter 17

HEADING TO MIKE MALKAN'S – 1:06 A.M.

We were on the way back to Van Leer's when Gancy's phone buzzed. She answered it, listened and said "Yessir" too many times for my taste and then shut the phone.

"Somebody saw Huggy tonight," Gancy said.

That made the soggy and bruised and flu-ish me sit up.

"Where?" I asked.

"Inside a bistro called Malkan's on 79th Street."

"That's no bistro," I said. "Especially during Christmas season. That's a rugby scrum."

"What's a scrum?" Gancy asked.

"When two teams jump on each other's shins and throats to get the ball. Somehow at Malkan's they got sex confused with bumping into each other. It's one of Manhattan's kooki-est saloons that way."

"How do you know it so well?"

"If you could look twenty-one, they served you," I said. "No questions. They made a fortune off us youngsters."

"You drank there?"

"I practically lived there. At sixteen, I thought that barflies, regulars and occasional hookers should be running America."

"And now?"

"Now I see why they don't let sixteen-year-olds run anything big."

"Who frickin' saw this gal?" Fox asked. "Wasting our goddamn time this way."

Drawing the gun and then having to cleanse himself with Chichak had shamed him. So now he was going to make it up by talking tough. I sighed. He reminded me of weak partners I'd suffered through in Patrol.

"There's that Bu car for the Chinese gal and her daddy," Gancy said. "Chichak wants them at the Command Center so that he can grill them."

Another car pulled up. Through the glass, I could see Levin and Smelka in the front seat. Levin beckoned to Lee and Beau Po.

Both Fox and Gancy needed a wake-up call to reality. I elected myself.

"That could have been your backup team," I said to Fox, low so that Gancy could not hear me. "With another team and some luck, you would have that unknown in front of you right now, getting all undressed."

"For such a loser," he said, "you are sure an expert on what everyone else on the earth should do."

His voice filled the car.

I could not let that one go by.

"What have I lost?" I asked. "All the stuff that you have?"

"Let's knock off the bull session," Gancy said. "We need some names and statements to fill up a 302 before we can put Bigmouth here where he belongs."

A 302 was obviously a report form of some kind.

On that cheery note, I watched Lee and her Daddy Beau vanish inside the dark back seat of the Bureau car. The Daddy seemed to take everything with detachment. Nothing bothered him. He just nodded his head and went along. He was probably old enough to remember the war with Japan when Chinese families ate zoo animals and millions of civilians starved.

My head kissed the headrest and stayed there. My eyes closed. I imagined Lee sitting next to me on this seat. The thought warmed my body's cords and unkinked them.

"Can Max hear us?" Gancy asked.

"He's out. God knows what is in his system to make him talk that way."

"Chichak should tell us who saw the victim," Gancy said. "Sometimes he plays it too close. That stresses me out."

"You know how he thinks on this frickin' stuff. He's told us this on other assignments. He wants us to have an open mind. Not to be biased towards any one person."

"His ideas don't work. We are a team, right? I'm wanting to transfer away from his by-the-book butt."

"Maybe that's why this Crackup agent is in his group," Fox said. "That's not just a coincidence. They train us not to believe in coincidences, right?"

"Just like psychiatrists."

"Right. Everything happens for a reason. Like, this Crackup agent feels that Chichak doesn't trust us. You and I gripe about it. But this fool cracks up."

"Jesus," Gancy said. "How many agents do you know who have killed themselves since the World Trade Center?"

"'course. A car-load. The stress hits us all. We screw up, and we may have a worse terrorist attack."

"And it's not just agents, either," Gancy added. "Radio dispatchers, translators, Special Support Group civilians and clerks. They feel the crunch, too."

"Remember Dayler?" Fox said. "He clowned his way through the Academy with me. Laughing, whiskey-drinking, Marine Corps sergeant and party animal. Loved working bank robberies in the Denver Field Office. Shot himself in front of his wife last Christmas."

"Hell, Fox, you could crack up right in front of me, and I might not know it."

"You should. You're the FBI."

"They don't train us for introspection, you know. Just some feel-good seminars at in-service training and those pamphlets that they love to hand out. They haven't updated those since I was sworn in."

"Well, S.A. Gancy, I'll make a deal with you. Let me know if you see me acting squirrely. And I'll do the same for you."

"Jesus, what if I'm too nutty to see that you're losing your marbles, too?"

"That is a problem. We could always bring a third person in on this deal."

"Negative on that. We're partners, right? We know and protect each other. You can't drag in a third person. It will screw everything up."

Pictures of gray Government hospitals, choked with wounded war veterans screaming at night, overworked kid psychiatrists and FBI agents who had slipped their anchors into cop stress hit me. The nights were longest there. I knew.

"You know, S.A. Gancy, you're right. And nobody normal would want to be the third person in a deal like that."

"You mean –?"

"Right, Gancy. Our third person, our referee, might be nutty himself to want such an arrangement."

"Well, if he's crazy, he won't be much help anyway."

"You know, it's scary to think that we are the best that America has."

With my eyes closed and playing possum, I toyed with the idea of offering myself as their third person, to watch over their frail sanity.

But that would not work, either. They would never trust anyone outside the Bureau.

CB

"Here we are," Gancy said. "Malkan's Bistro."

Malkan's was on 72nd Street, not far from the East River. It lay in between a row of brownstones and a superette that sold coffee and munchies to the drunk prep school kids lurching out of Malkan's. A painted bright red wooden motif surrounded the smallish front window. Discretion was advised here. Mike Malkan did not want parents able to spy on their offspring from the street.

My head shaking, I pretended to be waking up. They would not want me overhearing their little sanity chit- chat.

"Was I asleep?" I mumbled. "Here we are. Malkan's! A machine for printing money. The drinks are way overpriced. A hamburger costs you more than a windbreaker."

"The legal drinking age in. New York is 21 now," Fox said. "How does this frickin' place get away with serving minors?"

"Paying off the local flatfoots," Gancy said.

"Probably not," I said. "Malkan's is too discreet to make trouble. I think that it stays open because the Playpen mommies and daddies trust Malkan's to let their kids cavort and run around and make fools of themselves here. And not some dangerous bottle-club uptown in Harlem. These parents have juice. They want Malkan's open to protect their kids. So everyone cooperates. They served me when the legal age was eighteen and I was a pimply fifteen-year-old mess."

"You're older now."

"But like everything in the Playpen itself, there is a dark side to Malkan's."

"What's that?" Fox asked. "Recreational cocaine?"

"Something more classic. All this youthful innocence and cash attracts older men. They like drinking in kiddie bars because it makes them feel young. And they come on as wise veterans of the world. They might talk a youngster into bed here. They need patience, good clothes and a line of patter."

"The older men do all that for sex?" Fox asked.

"No," I said. "They have other plans beyond that. They may have business worries in sales, construction or owning their own little bar. They know that if they can marry some innocent young Playpen heiress, their cash-flow problems are over for life. That's the gold mine that some of them try for."

"They must be crazy," Gancy said.

"No. They're hustlers. And they live and hustle with the hope of making that one big score. That one big score could be a Playpen marriage."

"Come on," Fox said. "The Upper Crust is too smart to let a conman like that into the family."

"The Playpenners sure think they are," I said. "But con-men work them successfully all the time. Stock swindles, real estate schemes and everything else?"

"He's right about that," Gancy said. "I've investigated a millionaire home loan case which was exactly the same thing."

"Most swindles never get reported," I continued. "The victims are too ashamed. They will lose respect, prestige and authority. Other executives may stop trusting them. So they never tell your outfit."

"For the first time tonight, you're making sense," Gancy said.

"I don't buy it," Fox said.

"Most Playpenners are convinced that they are the origi-nal cat's ass," I said. "Brilliant, sharp, hard-driving executives. The truth is, most inherited what they got. Without their family wealth and high-powered connections, they could not function independently for three days in a row."

"Why are you boring us with this?"

"Because thugs like the ones staking out Malkan's sneak into the Playpen. And one could be our kidnapper."

"What else, Max?" Gancy asked.

She was good at letting me talk and make her job easier. Or maybe she was falling in love with me. The idea made me smile.

"Sometimes Daddy will see that his daughter's getting se-rious over the wrong kind of man, fifteen-plus years older than her. Daddy may offer the man five K to re-locate to Vegas. Or have his lawyer or head of corporate security contact the hustler and report back when the problem is removed."

"Why Vegas?" Fox asked.

"Because all he cared about was money. The hustler can go to Southampton, Miami or somewhere else and try again."

"You sound like this is your territory, Max," Fox said. "Are you one of these hustlers?"

"Not with my wardrobe. Or my stomach. They won't go for it. But most nights, there's at least one hustler hanging out here looking for a mark. I'll point him out to you."

"We'll sense him without your help."

"Right," I said. "Just let me go in first. And alone. I'll build a drink. Give me five minutes on my own. Then you come in. Don't go official unless you have to. And I need thirty bucks to get things moving."

They stared at me.

"I'm putting in a chit for this," Gancy said. "You owe me big time for this, Max. So does the victim. Here's twenty. Now, I'm really involved."

"Make it forty. It's way pricey in there."

"I can't believe this," Fox said. "You're telling us what to do again. Like you're a genius boss."

"I am neither," I said. "But we want to work this bar as fast and as thoroughly as possible. So we can get back to real work, right?"

"Following orders," Fox said.

"So you're lucky to have me here."

"Lucky," Gancy said.

"Because all bars move differently. And I happen to know how this one does."

"That's enough bull-crap bar talk out of you," Fox said. "Let us get to work, for Chrissake."

Chapter 18

INSIDE MIKE MALKAN'S – 1:23 A.M.

The bar ran about twenty-five feet. Four booths promised more privacy. My pal, Ace, used to sit here with me at under-age seventeen, pounding down rivers of beer.

If Huggy had been there tonight, so had Joan of Arc, Moby Dick and Richard Milhous Nixon. But my hands came up like an old boxer covering his chin and throat as I stepped inside.

The heat greeted me like an old friend after the chilly passage from the Bureau car to Malkan's entrance.

Despite the blizzard outside, the bar was packed with youngsters bumping into each other with that holiday feeling. Christmas was coming, after all, and this was the vacation time before gray January settled down upon all of us.

Though there was freestanding room at the back of the bar, the prepsters crowded around each other in the front, woofing words and tossing down cactus green bills.

Shrewd bar-hopping meant talking immediately on my entrance. If I waited a fraction of a second, my audience would wonder why and start listing my faults.

"Shelter from the storm?" I asked a wide and giggly young woman nearest the door. "'tis colder than the heart of a trollop out there on the frozen tundra."

"Exactly," she said, laughing at nothing much in particular. She had the whiny Valley Girl accent that some evil demon had created to plague our ears. I was hoping to live long enough to see those speech patterns go extinct.

Music from the sound system covered some of the group's shyness. In the song, the singer seemed to feel that nobody understood him. That would never do. So he was giving throat to his difficulties.

"What's a good drink for a frozen footsore traveler?" I asked, letting her mother me.

"Mexican coffee, with Kahlua and cream."

Seven or eight others were ranging up and down the bar. They were railing at each other but still paid attention to me out of the corner of their eyes.

The bar smelled of Beef Wellington that a lucky couple was eating at the table nearby.

Hoping that Fox and Gancy could wait a bit longer before coming in, I scanned the crowd.

Someone I suspected was a hustler stood laughing with three kids at the end of the bar. A slim, dark-complected Irisher in a charcoal suit, no tie and white dress shirt. He was presenting himself as a businessman but still a flexible and friendly guy, able to talk with anyone.

His expensive haircut said that he could spend money on appearances. But his voice marked him as not being from the Playpen. There was an underlayer of Queens, Brooklyn or perhaps Staten Island in his accent. His words sounded noticeably different from the private school voices all around us.

Irisher had probably discovered the Playpen in his twenties, I figured, and rented a modern one-bedroom place near here for a business deal or a quick seduction. There would be an ex-wife and a couple of kids back in his home neighborhood. He would send them checks whenever his freelance consulting operation allowed.

"Never saw this much snow come down so fast," he was saying. "In the service, they put me in Minnesota where it fell like this all the goddamn time. They wanted me to re-enlist, but I said I was going to Hawaii just to thaw out."

The veteran bartender, Basil, was a crusty ex-cook now trained to say "Sir." He stood about six-three, was growing a paunch and had been here at least six years to my memory.

Nobody in Malkan's knew my former sub-profession.

"This Mexican coffee shows that you have good taste," I said to the same young woman near the door. "My name's Max."

"Alexandra," she laughed.

"And this Mexican coffee puts me in the right mood for tonight's work," I said. That was no lie.

"What do you do, Max?" She was being the direct modern woman. She smelled of Scotch whiskey and clove cigarettes.

"In Mexico, I used to train young boxers. Now, that I've mellowed, I teach Spanish."

"In school?"

"No, thank you. Those days are dead and gone, thank the Lord. Regimentation, taking roll call, yuck."

"I know what you mean."

"Private students now. In fact, that's why I'm here. I'm supposed to meet Kate, but she's off sniffing paint thinner with her friend Huggy or some such tomfoolery."

"They're doing what?"

"I don't know, and I don't much care. This Huggy, or whatever her name is, is not my student. Kate is. Huggy's just gacking up my night. I'm supposed to meet this Huggy here tonight to get Kate's homework, or I don't get paid. I need the cash because I am going on holiday to Nicaragua tomorrow, and I don't even know what Huggy looks like."

"I'll find out for you," she said.

She turned to the two prepsters who were congratulating themselves on how drunk they could get doing shots.

"Do you know anyone named Huggy?" she asked.

They did not. But they asked the next clutch of students. It was like watching people play the old game of Telephone.

Alexandra seemed hyperactive. She buzzed around the bar.

Gancy and Fox made their adult entrance. A hefty kid with rare red cheeks under curly black hair slammed into them in passing. Hopefully the kid did not feel their Glocks under their coats. Another girl bumped them with her body. They did not mean to do it. It was just the Malkan's way. I hoped that the Bureau had trained them to hold their tempers slam-dancing with preppies in ritzy saloons.

Alexandra hipped her way past me.

"I'm making progress," she said. Many Playpenners knew each other. That was all that they knew. That was their entire social network.

Time dragged. The music and loud talk felt like nails pounding in my ears.

Fox was pumping Basil the bartender about why the prepsters liked Malkan's so much, doing a smooth subtle job from what I could hear. Maybe I had misjudged the man.

Alexandra came back, bumping into her best friends and tugging along a thin red-haired girl who looked like she wanted to be home in bed instead of talking to strange older men.

Wires gleamed on her teeth. Her bare arms showed orange freckles against the pale skin. She swayed her hipless body as if she wanted to run from me. Her eyes darted around the bar. She seemed afraid to stand still in one spot but did not seem to want to move either.

"Max, I did it!" Alexandra beamed. "It's Statistics 101. Everyone knows someone who knows a mutual friend of someone else. This is Elsie, and she knows Huggy. Elsie, I told you what he said about Huggy doing paint thinner and all, you know. I mean, really. I don't believe that Huggy does paint thinner," she said. "But, with the problems that she has, she should try it."

"You mean the family stuff?"

"Just exactly what I mean." She widened her mournful baby blue eyes. "I don't even know her all that well. But I do know when she's got troubles."

"Are you really a Spanish tutor?" Another prepster asked me, stepping over.

He was bigger than I and he seemed to know it. Side-burns sharped down his rough-cut face. A foreign accent burred his words. He looked about twenty-four, old to be pounding down drinks at Malkan's.

"Don't I look like one?"

"What you look like is some dirty old man trying a line of bull to hit on young chicks. Maybe I'm going to put you out into the snow myself. Do you want to die?"

Chapter 19

FARMING THE BAR FOR TALK – 1:35 A.M.

"Do you want to die?" he repeated.

Basil the bartender looked away with an expression that I could not decipher.

From my eye's edge, I saw Gancy and Fox tighten their bodies into confrontation positions. But they did not understand preppies.

The big fella was showing off.

"Are you Cuban, sir?" I asked him in Spanish. My feet eased into a boxing stance, without him noticing. If needed, two body shots would fold him right up. I just hoped that he would not throw up recycled cocktails all over me.

"So what?" he answered in Spanish. "What's wrong with that? You gonna make trouble about that?"

"I could tell by your accent. You can tell that by my accent that I teach Spanish. Look at my eyes and hair. I'm sure not Latino."

"I can't tell anything by that," he said. He burped. He was pretty well plastered. "We're going to fight. Because you're lying about teaching Spanish. You just speak college Spanish."

"You think so?" I pointed to the curly haired boy with rosy cheeks bumping into newcomers. My shoulders loosened to throw the punches.

I said a phrase in Spanish.

He stared at me, threw back his sideburned head and laughed. He kept laughing. Drunks acted quirkish sometimes. Every barfly knew that. His support system of prepster friends and regulars looked at him and then at each other.

Agents Gancy and Fox eased up and went back to talking with the kids.

The sound system played some unending dirge from a blues singer moaning about his sweet potato who had shucked him off. I did not blame her.

"What did you say to him?" Alexandra asked. "I never saw Pedro laugh like that before."

"Just a little Spanish expression," I said. "Between us men."

"Oh, goody. Please tell me."

"You're not old enough yet."

"When will I be old enough?"

"You'll never be old enough," I said, turning to the redhead. "Elsie, my dear, for the first time in a long while, I'm worried about money. My money. So I need your help to get my due."

She did not smile or react in any way. This was going to take some soft-shoe and some tap dancing.

"Man, let me tell you," Pedro the big preppy said. He wheezed and tears gleamed from his coffee-colored eyes. "No goddamn gringo ever used such an expression to me before. My family left bastard Castro's Cuba just a few years ago, my school records got lost, so I'm goddamn older than all these kids in my class. And I've been around already. Cuban women, you know?"

"I hope to."

"So I feel responsible for them. Especially when a stranger, much older –"

"Thank you."

"– comes in here drinking and playing around. Maybe you're a serial killer."

"Or a horn bug," I said.

He shrugged questioningly.

"Brooklynese for a sexual deviate."

"So they don't know nothing," Pedro said. "So I got to look out for them. You know?"

"I feel the same way," I said. My hand risked a backslap on his muscled back. "Two Catchers-in-the-Rye."

Gancy was flowing along the bar well.

She and Fox were forced to enter Malkan's together. Otherwise, everyone would notice three adults entering within ten minutes of each other and suspect something.

So they had come in together. But they had split up immediately. Some barfly couples did that. They would enter together and then seek strangers for entertainment, engaging in witty chitchat like F. Scott and Zelda Fitzgerald.

"What may I offer you to drink, Elsie?" I asked, playing her name like a salesman.

"If I drink, I throw up."

"Then we should wait on that. They have a pretty good Caesar Salad here. Or anything that you may want."

There was no way that she could hurry through a Caesar Salad. Nobody could. Maybe a beaver high on espresso could do it.

She thought about it.

Time seemed to hang.

"That sounds okay," she said. "It's good to have someone to talk to. I mean, really."

"You have your friends here," I said. "They'll be your closest friends for life."

She did not say anything.

"It will be okay, Elsie. I went through it, too."

I ordered the Cesar Salad from Basil the barkeep, then returned to our table, where I tried to relax Elsie the Effervescent.

It did not seem possible.

My third Mexican coffee helped me immensely. I wanted to take a nap.

By this time, Gancy had latched onto the same hustler I'd seen before. She was playing it friendly, and she had him laughing. It was a good smart move on her part. Either it was her FBI Academy training. Or she was a natural flirt. I would have to ask her later.

If I took that nap now, I might wake up on a warm morning in June in jade-green Central Park with dew still staining the leaves. That fantasy was better than this reality.

Fox went past us and jerked his chin towards the men's room. Maybe he was worried about me burning up Gancy's forty dollars.

I excused myself and stepped to the men's room.

Leaving Elsie was risky. She looked as if her shyness might swim back and take control over her. She might get that Caesar Salad to go and leave me with an empty place setting for dinner. In the past, I had often suffered the condition known as date loss.

∞

Inside the wood-paneled men's room, Fox waited until a prepster finished caterwauling on his cellphone about a party at Dutch Door's mother's apartment. Then we were alone.

Fox smelled of beer and bar nuts. Specks were stuck between his teeth.

"We're not getting anywhere here," he said. "Let's wrap this up and bag this sucker."

"If that means 'leave,' you're premature," I said.

He grumbled that I was of uneven parentage.

"You're doing a sweet job of getting Basil and the others to talk to you," I said. "Gancy's feeling out the obvious hustler, and I'm learning about the victim's family."

"We can get that off our computers."

"You think so? You can't get what I'm hearing off any computer. We're gathering useful info, Fox. That's what breaks hard cases, right? So don't stop the music now."

"I say we're going."

"Why? Because the sweet missies are not kissing your hand? Take your time with this, Foxy. It's worth it."

"If you don't come –"

"I know. You'll arrest me. That's counterproductive, Fox. An arrest means courtroom testimony. All the agents who don't like you to start with will take potshots at you about this arrest. You don't want that on your record."

"Chichak will back me."

"Chichak's retiring soon," I said. "You're not. This arrest will follow you around like a poisonous oil slick. Don't make a mistake tonight."

The fear of standing out from the herd showed on his face. FBI agents were not loners. They were club types, organization people.

Stepping past him, I left him to his worries.

ભ

Elsie was looking around at her friends bumping into each other at the bar. It was like a group hug.

Sitting down again reminded me that my pants were still wet from the snow.

"Oh, that Kate," I said. "And her ditzy pal Huggy. What a wombat name, 'Huggy'. What's her real name?"

"Wilhelmina Huggins."

"Then I don't blame for choosing that nickname," I said. "I would, too. Do you think that I would make a good Wilhelmina?"

She shrugged. It went on like that for a while. She tried not to say anything. It seemed that shyness was hammering her into silence.

Her salad came, and she gnawed on it.

In between bites of the parmesan and croutons, she filled me in on the Van Leers. Unlike most youngsters, she remembered where Cyrus had worked before his current job. And she dug in her memory to dredge up what castle-with-a-moat they had lived in before. That castle had doormen. Tomorrow, if I was still free, I would stop by and use come clever ruse to pump the doormen about the Van Leers. But at the moment, trying to think up a clever ruse hurt my feverish head.

"We went by 81st Street, and Huggy said 'That's where my mother goes to see her psychiatrist."

"Well, that's nothing these days," I said, playing the tolerant old uncle. "Everyone needs a bit of flying time on the couch of some Freudian expert."

"But her mother acts really weird sometimes."

"For example?"

"Sometimes she cries really easily."

"Then I need a psychiatrist, too."

"And she stays in her room for days and days," she said. "Do you want to hear a funny story about the Van Leers?"

"Why not?"

"Bess was two grades behind me, in fifth grade. Huggy told me this story. Bess's absolute, best, super friend in the world was Lindsay Lorting. In summer vacations from Miss Whippo's, they missed each other. When they separated, they would weep. So the parents decided that Bess should visit Lindsay at their high-end summer home in Antigua. To settle details, like airfare and outings and prices of things, the parents met for drinks at the start of summer. There would be fishing trips and seafood festivals and the like and so the parents agreed that $2,000 would cover it."

"She wasn't going Greyhound," I said.

Elsie ate by working around her plate clockwise, keeping the same slow tempo.

"$2,000 was the agreed upon figure, at this way-civilized meeting with drinks. Ten-years old, Bess was counting the days to go. She went and had an awesome blast of a time. When Lindsay's parents sent Bess's dad the bill, it was for $3500. They had slipped in an extra $1500.

"Huggy's dad went bonkers. But nobody ever said anything. So civilized that you could puke. After all, their kids are super best friends. Did he want to ruin that? The parents would have to keep smiling and stuff at parties. So he paid up, the whole silly bill. Bess said that making a stinkeroo over a piddling little $1500 would hurt Huggy's dad's worse than anything else."

"How?"

"They would call him cheap. Or they would say that he misunderstood the deal at the cocktail meeting. That he was not a good businessman if he could not negotiate a simple arrangement like that. After all, don't you absolutely know it would just be his word against Lindsay's dad's word?"

"That's a nice example of life's values to teach young people," I said.

"You know how grownups are."

"I'm learning. I wonder how many kids Daddy Lorting has. If he has four kids and he does this swindle with his four kids every summer, he'll pick up $6,000 per year."

"You're being way silly."

"If he could train his offspring to be extra-friendly to other kids and make them best friends, he might really make a killing in the kid market. This same racket could work during spring break and Christmas vacation. He's got to start thinking big."

"Nobody talks like that," she said.

"So Cyrus, Huggy's dad," I said. "He is the kind of joker who will just take it lying down, huh?"

"Well, what would you do?"

"Tear off his pricey silk underpants at the corporate Christmas party."

"Huggy's dad is all about appearances, appearances, appearances. You see how many dry cleaners there are around here? Each block has two or three. He's always picking up or dropping his shirts or his suits at a new dry-cleaning place. He wants his clothes to be just so. If you ask me, that's kind of freaky-deaky control craparoo. Other daddies don't do that."

"What else about him, Elsie?"

"Then Huggy's dad was downsized at his job last year. It was quite vague, really. Business talk just flies out of my air head. But I know that he had to borrow money from his mother, just to keep up those appearances."

"How much?"

"I don't recall, actually. But it was a lot."

"Borrowing from Mom is usually the final step," I said.

"Final step before what?"

I gave an eloquent shrug.

"I really shouldn't be telling you these things," she said. "It's just that I keep coming here, to this Malkan's, where everyone is supposed to have such a blast, and it just bores me. I mean, really."

"I know."

"I'm not smart, and I'm not pretty, and it scares me talking to strangers who give me bad vibes. But you don't scare me. And you're not boring."

She fidgeted and concentrated on her salad.

"I shouldn't tell you these personal things about Huggy," she said.

"Yes, you should."

"Why?"

That stopped me. Chichak did not want anyone to know about the kidnapping. Maybe Elsie still had things to tell me.

She looked over at her friends, still carousing and bumping into each other.

"This is starting to feel a bit weird now," she said. "I'm going. Good night."

"Half a minute, please, Elsie," I said.

She was standing up and reaching for a heavy tan Afghan coat with a red fur collar. Nobody had told her that redheads should not wear red.

"Huggy is in trouble," I said.

"Oh, yeah, right. Just because I'm young, you think that I'll believe anything."

"This is the truth," I said. "Neither you nor I hear it very often, but this is it tonight."

She paused.

I turned the full force of my look on her and tried to get through to her.

"Please let go of your coat," I said. "I need your help to find out if she was in here tonight."

She shook her head.

"How can you be sure?" I asked.

"She wasn't here. I've been here since six or so. Huggy doesn't come here much. She says that it's phony. Her sister Bess hangs here all the time."

"That tells me something about Bess."

I borrowed her pen and scribbled my cellphone number on a napkin.

"Tomorrow afternoon, you call this number. I'll try to settle my cellphone bill by then. At least, I'll have your number. I'll explain this whole mess, this whole goat rodeo, to you."

She sat back down again, still holding her coat. She talked about schooldays at Miss Whippo's and how their families played tennis together. I sat there, taking it all in, along, drinking my next Mexican coffee with S.A. Gancy's buy money.

"Elsie, do you remember when you first met Huggy?"

"I heard about her colors test before I actually met her. I mean, that's another freaky-deaky story. We all got this test for describing colors. It was the basics, you know? Red, white, green, purple."

"Being sisters, Huggy and Bess sat near each other. Huggy did not know her colors. She put down the absolute wrong ones.

"But Bess cheated! She sneaked looks at Huggy's paper and wrote down the wrong ones and got caught doing it by the teacher. When Bess got found out, she went ballistic and started hitting Huggy and the teacher.

"Bess's face got all red and crying and crazy like. Miss Whippo suspended her. Can you imagine suspending a six-year old? Our teacher and I took Huggy to the nurse, to make sure that she was all right. I didn't know Huggy much before that. But we started talking and became friends."

"That's a hard scene to forget," I said.

"Can I call you, just to talk about things?" she asked. "Not about Huggy, but other stuff? A girlfriend of mine has dropped out of sight. Okay?"

Chapter 20

DIGGING FOR APPLES – 1:56 A.M.

We drove back to Van Leer`s in silence. My thoughts crowded each other. My brain slid into combinations and permutations, I was trying to outthink the kidnapper. Playing "What If" games.

"If I do this, that will happen," I speculated. "But if I do that, this will happen."

My thoughts crowded each other. I needed to ponder.

When we arrived back at the Van Leers, I had to be shaken awaken by S.A. Gancy.

We looked at each other. Getting older and dozing off embarrassed me.

ೞ

Upstairs in the Van Leers, a white-haired woman wearing red and green Christmas colors was talking about how wonderful her vacation to Belize had been.

My weak eyes blurred and teared, coming from the cold to the warmth. My contact lenses burned. Fingers dashed a tear away.

She seemed to be hungry for an audience but was losing hers fast.

"It gave me a whole new perspective on life," she said. "Exactly what a vacation is supposed to do."

"A very dangerous country to visit," a gruff old gentleman in white tie and tails said in a British accent "Drug murders all the time."

"I didn't see any of that," she said.

The gruff gentleman inclined his bald head and moved on. So did the fringe of others, including my friend Preston and the man with the Santa Claus pin in his tuxedo lapel.

"That gentleman who just spoke up," the woman said. "He says that he is an English baronet."

"Oh, really?" I said, rubbing my eyes.

"But he isn't. He fibs about it."

My blurry eyes looked around the oil paintings and hand-carved furniture. The surroundings looked a lot better than the guests' manners did. This paradox had confused me ever since I was a ten-year-old boy, on scholarship in a wealthy school.

It was time for me to get intimate with this stranger.

"Whenever I am down there in Belize, my cellphone goes limp," I said.

"Not mine," she said. "Crystal clear reception, even on windy days."

The others drifted away. But I wanted something and stayed, head cocked towards her in respectful attention.

"It's good that you say that," I said. "Because Mr. Van Leer wants me to order another case of his favorite wine from my employer."

I did not dare risk mangling the pronunciation of Chateau Whatever-It-Was, as she looked like the type to pick up the fact that I was winging it.

"We can't use the landline. You understand why."

"Yes, of course," she said.

She was faking. She had no idea why we could not use the brownstone home phone. I realized that she was one of these drinkers who can put up a good front when they are too sloshed to hit the ground with their hats.

"Aren't you some kind of suspect or something, dear?"

It cost her something to be that direct.

"Oh, not anymore," I said, trying to be as casual as she was trying to be. "That was a misunderstanding. It's been cleared up for hours."

"That's good," she said.

"If I may just borrow that wonderful phone and see how it works to place the order," I said.

She was starting to have doubts again.

"Well, if you think that you should," she said.

"Sure thing," I said, sliding the phone from her grasp.

Breathing fast, I punched in my lawyer's cellphone. It said something bad about my personal life that I had this number memorized.

The owner watched me through half-closed bloodshot blue eyes. She even smiled a bit.

"I'm Marsilla Drayton," she mumbled. "But you didn't tell me your name."

"Max Holden Caulfield."

She was too full of herself to listen. In the Playpen, nobody listened to your answer.

"Who is this?" Simon asked.

"Simon, It's me." I said.

"What now, Max? Do you know what time it is? I'm trying to digest my family warm-up dinner. I was asleep."

"About that case of wine," I said. "It got stolen here in my van, and the customer is blaming me."

"Your message said 'David Balfour.' Thank heavens for high school English. He's the hero in *Kidnapped* by Robert Louis Stevenson. So you're saying that someone got kidnapped there?"

"Yessir," I said. "And taken in my van. They will probably want cash. Federal gentlemen here want everything from me."

I gave Marsilla a smile meant to reassure.

She took my hand and squeezed it.

"You're still delivering liquor in the Playpen," Simon-the-lawyer said. "So I assume these people are wealthy."

"Assume away."

"Then you had best cooperate fully. You say 'Federal gentlemen'. In a kidnap, that means FBI."

"I believe those were the letters. Yes."

"The FBI's lost a lot of its good reputation recently," Simon observed. "They'll want to make it up by acting decisively on a rich folks' Christmas kidnapping. If you impede them in any way, they'll charge you with hindering their investigation. That's an easy five-year sentence."

"Oh, dear," I said.

Apparently, Marsilla felt wonderfully reassured. Her powdered perfumed head lolled forward and onto my shoulder. She rested it there. It felt like a bowling ball on my collarbone.

"And if the kidnapper escapes, or they kill him in a showdown," Simon said, "they'll charge you with being an accessory before the fact. That covers them against charges of incompetence. The dead man cannot clear you by his testimony. And your record as an NYPD cop fired for 'By Virtue of Mental Disease' is a good fit for kidnapping the rich. God knows you always rail against them."

Right on cue, Marissa started to snore.

"I just want them to leave me alone," I said.

"That won't happen tonight," he said.

"If you only knew," I said. "Especially right now."

"Cooperate fully with them or I won't be able to help you."

"I left word for you to have the Playpen Irregulars look for my van. Ford F-150, nineteen years old, green, New York AHY-0303. Let me know where they find it. I'm at Van Leer's brownstone. The address is listed."

"Somebody else called me about this, Max. We'll find you. But the problem is motivating your Irregulars to hunt a car in a blizzard. They are not the most dependable of people."

"You say so, Simon? Because you're of them."

"Thank you. I suppose."

"We got Patso Murray of the Paramedics, Honest John Leahy, the Bartender," I enumerated my Irregulars. "Nancy Pau, the Jade Empress, the modern painter; Rags Raybeck, the gypsy cab driver who loves to drive in storms, and a slew of other colorful types. They'll find my van. What else would they be doing in this weather?"

"Okay," Simon said. "I'll re-contact them and see what they've got. But no vigilante stuff. I can't be a party to that."

"Heavens to Betsy, no," I said.

Marsilla was still snoring away.

"You, old gal, are a real window-rattler," I whispered.

As gently as I could, I eased her head back against the cushions of the sofa. Taking the phone formed a temptation. But if she woke and missed her phone, she would raise the alarm against me. I did not want that.

I lay it gently on her lap.

☙

My feet felt like clophoppers as I eased back downstairs to the dining room overlooking the garden.

Chichak, wearing half-moon glasses, tapped out messages on a laptop. Other agents were talking about their interview results.

"Excuse me, Mr. Chichak," I said. "Do you have any word on my van?"

"No, we don't. You gave us the plate, but DMV said it has gone through too many transfers to trace. Not tonight, anyway."

"But you should check this neighborhood for it."

"Why?" he asked.

"Because the gas gauge was on Empty. This was my last run of the night."

"You didn't tell me the gas was low," Chichak said.

"Yes, I did," I said truthfully.

"I don't remember you saying that at all."

We looked at each other.

Chichak looked about ten years older than my forty-six. Whenever two detectives over forty disagreed over who remembered what, things could turn nasty. When you were a young cop, you were sure and secure about your memory. That eroded with age.

Chichak's eyes held that knowledge about memory.

"So the kidnapper will have to restrain the victim with one hand and get gas with the other –" he said.

"– without anyone noticing," I finished his sentence for him. "All by himself. And there's a gas pump on 63rd Street and another on 96th. Nothing closer," I said. "So he might still be in the neighborhood. With Huggy. Can't you search this area?"

Chichak looked crisper now and younger with this new lead.

"Yes, we will," he said. "I'll start some teams out now."

"Thank you."

Now the harder part would come. The snow was piling up outside in the garden. It covered the stonework and the fountain in the center.

There might be a shovel buried under that snow.

In the highest tradition of the winter NYPD, dating back to 1854, I built myself another generous bourbon in the kitchen, slammed it down and went outside in the garden.

Nobody, guests or agents, paid me any attention.

CB

There was no stick or rake available. So I would have to use my sneaker-clad feet first. If I found nothing, it would be my hands.

The snow was still whipping down like an angry Norse god. The air blew inside me. I shivered.

The garden was about two-hundred-feet long and seventy-feet wide. Twelve brownstones opened onto it.

"The important thing is to do this systematically," I chattered to myself. "Start with the garden corner closest to Van Leer's. And hope that he dropped the shovel there."

Being systematic was always hard for me. With this cold, wind and falling snow, it seemed impossible.

My sneakers kept tromping down the snow, feeling for the shovel with the arches. If it was a wooden shovel, breaking it would be counterproductive.

"Time for the light touch," I kept chanting against the wind. "This is some wild night, straight out of Jack London, here in the Playpen."

Once in a while, I saw Zorah, the Brazilian Free-Thinker pacing back and forth against the large picture window. Behind her, Chichak and his teams showed how professional they could act.

The window glare made it hard to tell. But I felt that she was looking at me.

She kept pacing.

I wondered about her.

The foot plan did not work. The snow was too deep, three or four inches already.

So I bent down, feeling all my injuries and flu bugs scream in protest. My hands dug through the powder snow.

Numbness skewered me.

My feet froze.

Going back inside would show them what I was doing. They would forbid me to keep digging. Chichak would play the heavy father and I would just have to be the teenager who rebels.

Every winter, a few homeless froze to death this way in the Playpen. It could happen on a night like this.

The voices inside my head kept saying that I was not homeless, not yet. But I only had about three months of rent money in the bank. After that, anything could happen.

My cherry-red fingers found something in the snow. It was a dark green plastic handle to a shovel. I left it there and lurched towards the Van Leer brownstone.

☙

I tried to re-enter the kitchen without attracting any attention. Snow was covering me, and my hands did a spasm whirl from the cold. The guests all eyed me. They did not look happy with my bringing the chill in with me.

Chichak was still with his computer cadre in the dining room.

"Come outside, Mr. Chichak," I said. "I found the shovel that the kidnapper may have used."

"May have used? Why are you so certain?"

"You could catch him and ask him," I said. "It could have fingerprints or his DNA on it. Even in the snow. You should have it photographed where it is now. Then process it for evidence."

Zorah picked up a long black, coat trimmed in fur and black suede. It matched her hair. She stepped towards the garden door.

"Excuse me, ma'am," Diascu said. "But you can't go out there now."

"Why not? I live just over there, two houses down. And I need my medicines."

"Let her go, Mr. Diascu," Chichak said. "We'll all go outside together. It's not a crime scene yet. It could be a kid's shovel, Max. You're just trying to distract us. Like before."

He led Zorah and me outside.

୪

"The more I see of this," Chichak said, "the more I'm tempted to lock you up."

"Goodnight, gentlemen," Zorah said, giving me a look.

She trudged through the snow. Her heels made Thwock! noises in the snow. "That shovel is nothing special, Max," Chichak said. "I knew that this was a trick to get me off track."

"Aww!" Zorah cried out. "Get my pills! I can't breathe. If I don't get those pills, I could die! Please help me!"

She flopped down in the snow.

Chapter 21

WHO NEEDS ASYLUM? – 2:20 A.M.

"What's the matter with you?" Chichak asked her.

"Ohhh, I can't say the name in English. Please! I need my pills!"

Zorah roiled in the snow. I felt like throwing up. My flu body could not handle this.

Chichak whipped out his phone, called 911 and gave our location.

Other agents came out. Zorah rolled away from them.

"Don't come near me!" she shouted. "My pills!"

"No ambulance," Chichak said. "The storm has shut them down."

He still held the phone.

"911 operator says to get the pills into her fast," Chichak said. "Diascu, please take her feet."

"Not him!" Zorah shouted. "None of them."

She pointed at me.

"Just him!" she wailed. "Nobody else!"

"Ma'am, he's a subject in custody!" Diascu shouted above her wails.

"Just him!"

"You kooks deserve each other," Chichak said. "Max, take her feet. Move it!"

I moved it. My heart pounded inside me.

Chichak helped me hoist her in a fireman's carry with her weight on his shoulders. We took her to the back door of another brownstone.

"It's not locked," she said. "Just push open the door and hurry, please!"

☙

We shoved our way into the patio and carried Zorah into the ground floor den done in tropical dark wood. The warmth covered all of us.

Baked bread smell wafted from the kitchen.

"Where are your pills?" I asked.

"I'm all right now," Zorah said. "Mr. Chichak, thank you so much. You may go now."

"Max comes with me," he said. "There are some issues that you are not familiar with."

"I don't care," she said. "He is now my guest and he may remain. I am a Free-Thinker and do not approve of how your government treats the individual."

I rubbed my hands over me, trying to warm up.

"Miss, he is in my custody now, and I'm a federal officer."

"Not in this house, I'm afraid," she said.

She switched on a light and pointed to a metal plaque on the wall. I had to get closer to squint at it.

Below the United States eagle were the words:

U.S. Department of State.

> Foreign consular residency. All persons
> should be advised that this residence is
> International Territory as defined by
> the Warsaw Pact of 1949.

"My sister is the cultural attaché from Brazil to your United Nations," Zorah said. "This is her house. You have no authority here. Unless you want an international incident about violating our rights, you will leave now."

I breathed in, shaking my head. A warmer feeling of relief came from my feet and flushed across my body.

"You, Free-Thinker, are rescuing me from the good gray government," I said. "I'm at liberty again."

Nobody paid me any attention.

"I don't want to arrest you for obstruction," Chichak said to her.

"Sir, I'm afraid that you still don't understand," Zorah said. "My sister's diplomatic immunity extends to me. No American policeman can arrest either of us. On any charge. All that you can do is lodge a complaint through your State Department and possibly get us recalled."

"I'll do that right now."

"The process takes weeks. Or months. If you want to check this, I have a U.S. State Department number for you to call."

Chichak flushed. The professional was being out-professionalled by this stunning Free-Thinker.

Something chewed at me. Chichak had walked into a setup where he could not win. That happened to cops all the time. He was a manicured executive, charging through life behind his FBI credentials folder. I used to hoist the silver biscuit of an NYPD shield in my bluejeans. So we had that much in common.

A thought corkscrewed through my head. It was a nutty one.

"I have my own number, thank you very much," he said to her.

Professionalism was breaking down, all right. He turned his tuxedoed back on her like a kid and retreated to a corner. He cellphoned another careerist and conspired in low tones.

Zorah slithered out of her coat. Being the guest, I hung it up for her. It smelled of her light perfume. I felt like taking her in my arms and diving into a bottle of it.

"You can stay here as long as you wish," Zorah whispered to me. "They may post detectives outside if you try to leave. Please consider yourself as my guest."

"You'll get in trouble for this."

"I think that you're worth it. Take a hot shower and then we can eat. Sleep as long as you like. Very thick blankets here."

"Sounds like heaven."

Her black eyebrows quirked.

"Better," she said.

My body was warming up, bit by bit. On a night like tonight, men would smash through doors and windows and break into homes just to curl up and sleep warm.

Chichak's voice went up and down.

Then he snapped the phone shut.

I was squinting at the U.S. State Department plaque. My tension was mounting nicely. I could see my own gut moving in and out from it.

"What's wrong with you?" Chichak snapped. "That sign speaks plain enough. Are you blind or something?"

"Legally, yes," I said. It was the truth. "Legally blind, according to New York State."

"How the devil do you drive a liquor delivery van when you're legally blind?"

"Very carefully."

"You are a mess. Prison would help straighten you out."

"Mr. Chichak, you have ascertained what I said," Zorah said. "It is time for you to go."

Chichak's fell back into Government-Robo-Mode.

"Yes, ma'am," he said.

"Wait up, Chichak," I said. "I have another idea."

"You always do."

"It's a wild one," I said. "You'll like it. I'm coming with you."

Zorah stopped in her tracks.

"Max, he'll put you in prison!" she said. "Are you crazy?"

"Everyone always asks me that."

"And with good reason, I believe now."

"Why?" Chichak could not bring himself to say my name. "You may find yourself facing a capital charge."

"I think that you're a better detective than that," I said. "There were a dozen times tonight when I could have run from you. A guilty guy would have fled. You know that I am not involved."

"But you're withholding something," he said.

"Everyone withholds something. Haven't you learned that yet?"

"This is not one of your jokes!" Zohra said. "This could finish you!"

Her voice cracked. I sucked in a deep breath.

"Hope not," I said. "But I'm going to do everything I can to get Huggy back safely. If that means prison, then I'll try to laugh my way through that, too."

"Max, I can't believe this," she said.

"That's me," I said. "Max, the Unbelievable Man."

Chapter 22

Preppy Runs Amuck – 2:37 A.M.

Chichak and I trudged through the snowstorm in the garden to Van Leer's home. The wind made talking tough.

When we got back inside, Chichak brought me to the kitchen and poured us two cups of steaming coffee from a white-metal and chrome percolator. The goose smell still hung in the air. My beaten body said that sitting on this stool was a wonderful idea.

"You know, Max, I've had helpful individuals assist me in investigations before."

"Like me."

"I wondered why they were doing it. In some instances, they basked in the reflected grandeur of the FBI."

"That lets me out," I said.

"Stop acting foolish. In other instances, they turned out to have mental issues. And they looked and acted as normally as you and I do."

"You, anyway."

"As a professional interviewer, I was shocked and embarrassed by how they had fooled me. Now, as regards us, is there some way that I can motivate you to identify yourself, and we can put this issue behind us?"

"Yes," I said. "Ignore me and work your case."

"That may be impossible. Because you may be the key to my case. And, with the best intentions in the world, you may not even know it. Is it possible that you may have recognized the kidnapper from somewhere?"

The guest's talk from upstairs took on that louder, liquored-up quality of a long night pounding down cocktails. Any bartender would know that tone.

Chichak was using an old interview tactic, to make me condemn myself. If I said that I DID recognize the kidnapper from somewhere, it would make me guilty of withholding information. A jury would see that as a sign of guilt.

Chichak's task now was to get me to admit this. Once I admitted that, he could open me right up.

"I never saw him before," I said. "He was a younger, jock-type fella who knew how to hit. Do I look like I hang around gyms?"

Chichak hunched forward, looking as concerned as a veteran salesman at Brooks Brothers trying to suit up a long-term customer.

"I may see a resolution to this," he said. "Please stay here for a bit. That coffee's good after the snow, isn't it?"

"I feel like taking off my shoes and diving into it."

He went away to speak with his agents outside in the foyer.

☙

Agent Evers came into the kitchen, hugging herself in a paper-thin raincoat. Snow still clung to her black hair and was melting to run down her face and neck. Her white lace dress showed under the raincoat.

"Special Agent Evers," I said. "You'll freeze outside in that frilly party dress."

She did not smile.

"Bureau," she said.

Then she left.

"That was cryptic," I said aloud in the empty kitchen. "Think that one over."

More guests came down. They filled the kitchen with their noise.

"We're all fretting that the kidnapper hasn't called back," my earlier pal, Patrician Eyeglasses, said.

"That FBI man said not to talk about it among ourselves," said a sweet-faced woman with high cheekbones and frosted hair cut short in a shag. "Maybe we should follow their directive."

"Is no neighborhood safe anymore?"

The Playpenners always felt themselves protected.

"We have all types of interesting people at this party," Santa Claus Pin said. "And tonight's crisis has brought us together."

"All different philosophies," Sweetface confirmed. "Like the characters in Thomas Mann's book *The Magic Mountain*."

"Or that other book," the man said. "*Ship of Fools*."

"That was Katherine Anne Porter," Sweetface chided them.

Chichak came back into the kitchen.

"Max, it's a little too public here," be said. "Let's go somewhere private."

"You're in charge," I said.

ରଃ

He brought me out to the foyer, turned left and opened a large door. It led down some wooden steps to the basement.

He switched on a light.

"After you," he said.

I stepped down the stairs with him right behind me.

The basement felt colder than the first floor did. A heater's noise bumped and whirred. The smell of fresh laundry mixed with an odor of old metal.

Nobody would be throwing Christmas parties down here.

I was already at the bottom.

The stairs creaked.

Chichak was going back upstairs.

"Hey!" I shouted.

His tuxedo back went through the half-open door. He switched off the lights and closed the door from the outside. The basement went black.

I heard the lock click shut.

ରଃ

"Hello again," a voice called from the darkness.

I froze on the steps. My hands curled into fists.

"It is I, Mad Dog," the voice said. His voice slurred from drinking. "I've grown up with the Van Leer family. When they need something, I will give it to them."

He was somewhere below me.

Knees bent, I jumped back up the steps to the door. Using momentum, I kicked at the door with everything that I could gather.

The door did not move.

I tried again.

My foot slammed harder.

"Don't bust yourself, Max," he said. "Didn't you know these doors were burglar-proof?"

His voice was getting closer.

There was no time.

My sneaker launched up towards his voice. I kicked out.

My right foot caught his chest.

He went back a step.

His hands brushed my foot.

He was going to squash me against the door and wall.

He had my foot now and twisted my ankle.

Fear froze me.

He twisted harder.

If the ankle snapped, he could finish me in seconds.

I pushed off with my hands. My side lay on the steps.

My left foot snapped against his leg. He fell back. So did I. We tangled and tumbled all the way down the steps.

My earlier bruises screamed for attention. I rolled across the stone floor.

There was a sunken pit on the floor. My hands felt it to be about five feet square. A building heater took up most of the pit.

To dominate him, I had to speak first.

"This is silly," I said, trying to drawl again like a veteran street cop. "You hurt me, and I feed you to the law. You'll go upstate for years and ruin your life."

He laughed. He did not sound worried at all.

It chilled me to hear it.

Threading off my belt in the dark, I moved away from his voice and closer to the pit.

My fingers found the boiler On/Off switch. I tied my belt to the conduit leading to the switchbox.

A clump of things lay in the dark near the boiler. A stack of heavy suitcases. I felt for a suitcase handle and tied the other end of my belt to it.

Now the belt was stretched taut.

My eyes had adapted to the dark now. I could make out shapes. I played for time, hoping that my vision would get better.

"Tomorrow, I can be at my family's time-share in Acapulco," he said. "Mexican police won't give a shit about a fistfight two thousand miles away."

"Is it worth that much to you?" I panted. Exhaustion and flu made my voice squeak. I sounded as if I was pleading with him. That feeling enraged me.

"Or I kill you down here," he hissed. "No police at all then. You were drinking, fell downstairs and broke your neck."

He jumped towards my voice. That was no surprise. He would headhunt me. That meant trying to take off my head with one of his power punches.

Kids like him always headhunted. They had never fought for real. Beginners always went for the head. But anyone with fight-time behind him knew what short sharp body punches could do.

His punch caught my cheek. But I was ready for it and already moving backwards.

His follow-up came, just like the movies. But I kicked. My foot tried for his knee. It caught the thigh instead.

He slowed. I kicked again. My foot hit the wall.

His punch caught my chin. It was blind luck. He kept swinging. The tuxedo material rasped as his arms flew through the air.

There was a trick that street fighters had taught me. If you stomp your foot hard and then kick with the other one, the recoil energy strengthens your kick. Don't ask me why.

It worked.

— 152 —

It worked on Mad Dog. My foot slipped from his groin to his thigh. But it got him mad. That was what I wanted. I was gambling with my life using my belt trick.

"Don't!" I said. "Please."

My weak strikes followed.

Then I did what no smart boxer should ever do. I backed up from his punches in a straight line. No angling off to the side.

That made it easier for him to keep hitting me. He did. His fists kept hitting my face.

My calf hit the belt. I lifted my numb leg. I stepped over the belt.

Lust for the bust took him over. He grunted like an animal mounting a female for rape. He could not stop himself. He came for me in a straight line.

My belt tied from the boiler switch to the suitcase was stretched tightly in front of him at shin level. He followed me.

Then he tripped across my belt and fell.

"Waww!" he shouted.

My belt must have caught him across the shins. He fell into the boiler pit. That was my plan.

His body hit the stone floor. Something KLONGED into the metal boiler. I hoped it was his head.

"You bastard!" he cried. "You tricked me!"

Talking would give him my location.

The boiler came on now. A dim red light showed. We could see each other a little now.

"You're dead!" he panted. "I'm gonna to ruin you."

Another idea hit me.

"Dream on, tough guy." I snapped. "Beat up a fat guy twenty years older than you. I bet you were the toughest guy on your lacrosse team."

Like I wanted, he rushed me. I was standing by the wall now, my side turned to him.

This had to be just right, or he would take my head off.

One hand caught my collar and spun me around. That was the set-up for his killer right-hand punch.

My head ducked down. I gave him the top of my head.

His fist smashed the top of my head. It hurt me. I staggered backwards. But I heard and felt his fist smash apart. His broken bones scratched my scalp Wet stuff splashed my cheek.

"Owww!" he wailed. "My hand! My friggin' hand!"

Like I had planned, his punch missed my face and hit my skull instead. An old boxing trick, called "giving your opponent a little skull."

"You did it to yourself, kid."

He rolled on the floor, crying.

I felt bad for him.

But I did not feel too much bad.

This basement was supposed to be my tomb.

Chapter 23

SHE WALKS IN BEAUTY – 3:02 A.M.

"Straighten up, Mad Dog," I said. "Hand me your cell-phone, please."

"No!"

"Maybe I shouldn't use the word 'hand'," I said. "So let me have it. You use it."

"No!"

"Drugs can kill your pain. They're on the other side of that door. Call Chichak."

"No."

"I don't even like saying Chichak's name. But he can open that door. So call him. I can take that phone from you, you know."

"Try."

"You're rolling all around the floor now. There's no point in putting it off. You're not going to live in this basement, are you?"

Tears had to have been kept streaking his face. He tucked his ruined hand under his armpit.

"Took a lot of guts to take me on and risk your investment banking or whatever career. You should have won. But fights are unpredictable. I used to train boxers in dirty tricks."

"I'm not letting you out," whimpered Mad Dog despite himself.

"If you don't get that hand in a cast pretty damn quick, it will cripple up. That's something else I learned. You've got what we call a 'boxer's fracture'."

"Without prompt care, you'll never use it well again. You've got parents. They'll need your two strong hands to lift them when they age. Don't cheat them out of it. They deserve you helping them."

He handed me the phone. I called the operator who put me through to the FBI Field Office. They would relay the message to Assistant Director Chichak.

Waiting was something I could do.

After a longish while, the door opened. I blinked in the sudden light and walked up the stairs to confront Chichak and Diascu.

"Surprised to see me walking, Chichak?" I asked. "Go scrape up your stooge. What did you want him to get from me? A confession or just my last name?"

Chichak looked at me with no expression.

"You've perfected the art of surviving in a bureaucracy," I said. "Saying nothing and feeling less."

He and Diascu passed me as they went down the steps.

ॐ

They brought Mad Dog upstairs. No guests were near the basement entrance. Mad Dog's blond face looked ripped in two by pain.

"Take him to Lenox Hill Hospital in my car," Chichak said. "Let him speak to the staff about what happened. Try not to identify yourselves unless absolutely necessary. Then get back here."

Hunching up against my injuries, I went out in the snowstorm and waited near Chichak's Cadillac. My wallet was still under the front seat. I wanted to jam it into my thick winter sock so that a frisk would miss it.

If the FBI found my wallet and idented me as a cop bounced for head music, they would jail me as an accessory. They would worry about court later.

If they jugged me, I could not help get Huggy back.

Feeling like a sneak thief, I tried the doors. They were all locked. Chichak mistrusted Manhattan.

Two agents, Smelka and the Latino one, came out with Mad Dog between them. Smelka switched open the doors by clicking the keychain device.

I ripped open the passenger door and groped under the seat.

"Hey, there!" the Latino agent said. "Get on out of there."

"Mr. Chichak wants me to go with him," I said. "Don't you remember him saying that just now?"

My fingers kept probing under the seat. No wallet yet.

"I don't remember any such damn thing."

"Mad Dog wants it," I said. "Right, Mad Dog?"

"Just get me there," Mad Dog said. "Let him come if he wants."

"Okay," Smelka said. "Who cares?"

He came around to open the back door. He eased Mad Dog in.

My fingers touched my wallet.

A stern voice crackled from the FBI radio.

"In years past, no FBI agent would ever sue the Bureau for discrimination," the voice said. "It was unthinkable. 'Don't embarrass the Bureau' was a law that we all lived by."

"There's our Crackup guy," Smelka said. "You, sir, out of this car."

"Why?" I asked.

"Get your hand out from under that seat," he said.

"Why? Maybe you should go kiss a duck."

"Because this is a boss's car with a Direction Finder on the radio. We can scan and find this fruitcake that way. But not with you in it."

"An FBI agent was the most respected worker in the country," the voice went on. "That respect made the average witness WANT to help us. Mr. Hoover personally inspected every Academy graduate to make sure that he looked like what the public expected in an agent."

I reluctantly got out of the car and into the snow.

"Why can't we recognize his voice?" the Latino agent asked.

"Because he's got some material, cloth most likely, over the mike to change his voice," Smelka replied. "Loudmouth old agents used to do that."

"Stop gabbing and get me to Lenox Hill, will you?" Mad Dog moaned.

The Cadillac took off.

I staggered back to the brownstone without my wallet.

೮෨

"Have you looked in a mirror?" a woman with bronze-colored hair asked me on the ground floor. "My goodness gracious, did somebody hit you?"

"Somebody wealthy, yeah. Without much goodness gracious."

She tilted her head upward as she frowned. Sweeps of her blonde hair fell heavily onto her pale features. She had a little girl's surprised face, with pouting full lips done in a pinkish shade. Her dress was a dark chocolate color .She moved her lean body like a rock-climber in condition. In scarlet high heels, she stood a few inches beneath me.

"And who are you, stranger?"

"I'm Francesca." Her speech was a whispery with a Boston accent. "I just got here a little while ago and everyone related to me what happened. So I thought that I should stay."

"Why 'should'?"

"Because I have a background."

"That sounds nicely vague," I said. "A beautiful mysterious woman. With a Past. You're not from this Playpen."

"This what?"

"Upper East Side here. Where everyone pays such high rent that real life never breaks through to intrude."

"How can you tell?"

"I have my ways."

"If you would please come here. I want to wash you up a bit. Some of those bruises look quite formidable."

"They are."

೮෨

She brought me into the kitchen, found hand towels, wetted them and patted the places where Mad Dog had hit me.

The towels came away bloody.

Her hands felt hardish, like someone who had worked with them a lot. She seemed to know that and used them as gently as possible. There was a ring of white gold on her middle left finger and a silver wristwatch on the same hand.

"I'm trying not to look at my bruises," I said.

"No. Look at me instead."

"If you insist. What did the Playpenners, the other guests, say about me?"

"I don't wish to cause you pain by saying this. But most don't like you."

"They are standing at the back of a long line."

"They feel that you helped kidnap Huggy."

"And what do you think?"

"One doesn't know what to think in something as complex as this. Only that you're a bit confused and need direction."

"And that's you? The Director?"

She broke into a smile. Nothing that I could say seemed to rattle her.

"I firmly believe that when things slow down for you, your path will become clear. All the problems that you have now, you can release them to a Higher Power and you will know what to do. I hope that we can speak like this later on tonight."

With that, she brought me upstairs to the second floor.

Chapter 24

INTIMACY – 3:28 A.M.

"Why later?" I asked. "The way that things are going fast right now, there may not be any later."

Up close, Francesca's eyes were a marvel of sea-green sensitivity.

"Why?" she asked. "Are you planning to do something?"

"I don't have to plan anything. Tonight is not a night for planning. Events just slam into me."

"How?" she asked.

"You've spoken to the other guests. They say that I'm the local rogue."

"Group judgments," she said. "They are seldom accurate."

"How long have you known the Van Leers?"

"Cyrus? About a year off and on. It was good of him to invite me to this party."

"Good for me, too. Please walk with me a bit."

"I don't want to leave the Van Leers just yet," she said. "They're in a very fragile state."

"Talk with me. Please. Because I can help get them back to the state that they were in, waking up this morning."

She gave the up-from-under look with those same eyes.

"I think that I see the right room over here," I said.

"Whatever for?" she asked.

"Privacy."

Trying to look serene and unruffled, the Detached Gentleman, my eyes danced around the rooms. Playpenners were still cocktail-chatting through the nearby places. I stepped down the hall. She hesitated and then followed me.

○ℨ

There was a smaller study off the hallway. Maybe Mrs. Van Leer used the room to handle the household accounts and deliveries and gardening services. Brownstones like this did not run on their own.

It had Tiffany lampshades, wooden armchairs and a roll-top writing desk. The decor meshed with the other ones in the house. Someone liked the Victorian cozy look for their rooms here.

Leather-bound books lined the small bookshelf. It smelled of furniture polish and clean cotton. Wooden surfaces gleamed in the low light.

Something about Francesca made me question everything that she said. Isolating her might bring that reason to me.

Or maybe I just wanted to be alone with her.

Once I stepped inside, Francesca pulled me closer and kissed me. I half- stepped back in surprise. She came in closer and gripped me.

The hug warmed my bruised flu ish body.

"Well, well," I tried saying. My voice came out scrambled.

"You're an interesting man, Max, Max —"

"Rumplestiltskin."

"Oh?"

"My friends call me 'Rumpy'."

"Oh, do they?" She smiled and leaned against my arm as if she were sunning herself on the beach on the French Riviera and had all the time in the world to languish. "Well, you'll excuse me if I don't call you Rumpy."

"You're excused."

"If Huggy gets returned and you get through this night unscathed, what will you do?"

"Well, the first thing," I said, "is to roll over and turn off the alarm clock because I'm probably dreaming. There's no way that I'm getting out of tonight with a whole skin, my Francesca."

"I'm not your Francesca. Not yet."

"What is your last name?"

"Maiden name or married name?"

I could feel the smile drying on my bruised mouth.

"Let's start at Genesis," I said. "The very beginning. The maiden name."

"I warn you that it will make you laugh."

"Tonight, I could use it."

"Douxgateau."

"That's quite a mouthful," I said.

"Thanks a lot," she said and kissed me again. "Growing up with it was a challenge. It means 'Sweetcake' in French."

"Is there a Mr. Douxgateau?"

"Of course. My father. Do you think that I was created by immaculate conception?"

"Not hardly," I said, disengaging her arms. "I meant the husband."

"Oh, him. He was a Marden. I divorced him last year."

My head cocked, looking her over again.

Her smile heated more.

"You like surprising me," I said.

"Why not? Games are healthy. So long as the players know the rules."

"What are ours?" I asked. "Since tonight, I have one foot in federal prison. And you may be planning tomorrow's brunch date, for all I know."

She came in closer to me then, giving me the full force of her eyes.

"I promise you that I'm not planning tomorrow's brunch date," she said.

"You said earlier that you had 'a background'. What do you mean by that?"

"I'm told some divorces are neat and amicable. Mine wasn't."

"Sounds like a speech that you rehearsed to spare yourself further pain," I said. "Street people use the same gimmick to explain why things go wrong for them. A charming whiskey-headed woman named Michelle in my building did that. I could hear her voice coming up the airshaft, singing out her mantra, 'Every time, I turn around, I'm going to jail AGAIN!'"

The cocktail party talk seemed far away now.

"As the Irish say, 'I'm sorry for your trouble'," I said.

"As am I," she said. "I had therapists and counselors coming through the windows to help me. I was a strong, independent woman before my marriage. I made the mistake of thinking I could somehow sidestep the pain so many others suffer in a divorce. At first, there was a roaring in my ears whenever I tried to sleep. And my pulse kept going ting! ting! ting! even when I tried to sleep. My gracious, but it felt like my body was a factory open all day and all night for manufacturing unhappiness."

"That's an odyssey," I said.

"And, I'm afraid, one with a very uncertain ending."

"You look very collected."

"That's the problem. During the divorce, I would reach a plateau of calm and say, 'Okay, Francesca, girl, you made it. You're through the rough patch.' And I would tell the counselors, 'Thank you. I'll call you if I need anything.' Then something, a feeling, a remark, would trigger my crying again. I would gush like a Tiny Tears doll. Without knowing why."

Footsteps sounded nearby. I disengaged myself from her.

"Why are you stepping away?" she asked.

"I don't know," I said. It was the truth. "You might be the last woman in my life that I kiss."

The footsteps got closer.

A couple whom I'd seen before passed by our study. The man held a glass half-full of Coca-Cola. It had to be Coca-Cola. These were not the types to put the kind of rum or whiskey they kept on hand in the same glass as Coca-Cola.

He had a saggy hound-dog face and gold-rimmed glasses under hair that was dying out in white wisps on his scalp.

She was wide and slow-moving, with faded red hair and soft arms in her skyblue dress.

She held a tin can of diet soda in her free hand and with the other held Mr. Gold-Rimmed's. They were in absorbed in each other as they went by our hidden spot.

He giggled and whispered in her ear. She laughed with him and brushed her hip against his tuxedo.

They kept moving down the hallway until the dark covered them up.

"They seem quite happy," Francesca said.

"They must be new to the Playpen," I said. "They haven't been wised up yet."

"There's that term, 'the Playpen', that you used before," she said. "Do you really believe that living in this sanctuary of quiet and safety robs you of the ability to be happy?"

"It seems to," I said.

"Not to me. If you could afford the best for your family, where would you want to live? In a slum, where everyone is at risk? Where your children might be raped? Traumatized by who knows who or what?"

I sat down in one of those comfortable leather chairs and spread my feet, a relaxation trick from Patrol. Whenever my street temper rose up in me, I would try to put distance between me and whoever had enraged me.

"Francesca, I'm listening to you."

Somehow, I was being lectured again.

"That couple has realized their dream of being fulfilled with each other," she said. "Without being young or handsome anymore. What do you think about that?"

"I don't know. That's starting to be my new slogan."

"I think that this use of the term 'Playpen' is your way of saying 'Look at me. I'm better than those rich people who need money and a comfortable life. I'm Max, and I have a meaningful life with low income and no wife or children to worry about, but I'm a free maverick spirit.' Have you been married, Max?"

"Just once."

"You see? Even that answer mocks people who have been through a death or a divorce and have the courage to try again. You think that you can look at these people in tuxedos and party dresses and know everything about their lives?"

"Probably not," I said. "Usually, I make mistakes on an hourly basis."

"For example –"

She assumed a schoolmistress pose of which I didn't think her capable. As she breathed in and out, her breasts rose and fell. I hoped she didn't notice me noticing.

"– I've walked on the streets with Cyrus. When filthy homeless people approach him for money, what do you think that he does?"

"I haven't the faintest," I said. Emotion made me sound croaky.

"He excuses himself to me, reaches in his pocket and gives them money. Then he asks their names and gives his. Some want to shake hands, but he demurs. For which, I am grateful. Airborne pathogens and things like that. But he makes a human connection with them and gives them what they need."

"What they want," I said. "Some are using his cash to buy crack and beat their significant others in their lives, if any."

"Cyrus says that he remembers having money worries, when he was younger."

"Any recently?" I asked.

"Of course. Who doesn't, Max? Only those who have given up on trying to help their families or have some sugar daddy in the background always ready to bail them out. Or the worst case, the drop-outs who wind up like you."

That stung me. I sniffed, feeling my eyes wet with hurt.

"This is starting to sound like an oratory with me praising Cyrus," she said. "But he also cuts checks to the Lenox Hill Settlement House. And the Coalition for the Homeless."

"Hold tight," I said. "How do you know Cyrus again? You're a beautiful divorced woman who has walked down a fair number of streets with him. You said so yourself. That's fairly rare around here, to be friends like that."

She smiled, and her face lit up again.

"I know Cyrus through some social programs we both support," she said. "I was serious when I spoke with you earlier about a Higher Power. We all must acknowledge that. Or else we will all flounder by our design until we discover that we are not so powerful. Is it your arm strength? The big car you're driving? Or your money? That makes you believe that you are so powerful?"

"Negative on those three," I said. "Or any criteria you want to pick."

She smiled sadly.

"But I see you as a very powerful person," she said. "I listened to you speak with those FBI agents and also with these guests, the ones you call 'Playpenners'. You would be able to do so much if you could harness that power and humor into the right channels. And you and I could do that together."

That last word hung in the air.

I wondered what self-help program or double-barreled Whatever-Anonymous she was about to pitch to me.

"That seems bizarre on your part," I said. "Why put your future in with me? Nothing in it for you."

"Oh, I think there is."

"Just to be prosaic for minute," I said. "How do you handle your landlord when he comes calling for the rent check?"

"You mean, what is my work?"

"That'll do, for a start, yes."

"I have my own real estate business. It's done quite well these past few years. Manhattan fluctuates, as you know. From time to time, I've taken chances on people whom I respect."

Time for me to say something brilliant.

"Yop."

She looked away. I felt that she thought I was a disappointment. Time for me to deliver another sparkling piece of wit.

"Is Cyrus happily married?" I asked.

"Of course."

"Why 'of course?'"

"My dear Max, I'm afraid you've been spending far too much time with sad, unfocused people. Cyrus and Cornelia seem quite fulfilled and happy to this outside observer."

"That should teach me to play detective," I said.

"I don't think that detectives want to hear about happy marriages. Not among the people that they're investigating. Only their own."

"Too late for mine."

"That was yesterday. Tomorrow is where your joy should be."

"Doesn't seem likely," I said.

"Ah, but it could be."

She leaned forward and pressed her mouth against mine.

We stayed that way.

The room started to spin.

Maybe I was holding my breath. In high school, I used to do that while kissing. It was time to break that habit.

Footsteps sounded nearby.

Chichak and his squad of underlings were tromping down the hall. They would pass right by Francesca and me.

I disengaged from Francesca and tried to look innocent. The FBI probably disapproved of kissing on general principles.

Runyon came up to Chichak. Runyon seemed to have lost some of his zest. His eyes hooded, as if he were just going through the motions.

"Mr. Chichak," Runyon said. "Do you have a moment, sir?"

Chichak took off his half-moon reading glasses to look at the agent. Francesca watched from the doorway.

"Not right now, I'm afraid," Chichak said in his stern fatherly tone.

From what I could see, these two changed their game with each other all the time.

"Not the right time at all," he finished.

Runyon glanced at the other agents to see if they had heard. His big neck muscles tensed against his white dress shirt. I could see them contracting.

When he spoke, his voice was at a lower pitch.

"Excuse me, sir," Runyon said. "Perhaps you forgot that you assigned me to liaise with Mr. Van Leer. He says that he needs to speak with you on a topic that can't wait."

"Certainly, Runyon," Chichak said. He buttoned his tuxedo over his hip-holstered Magnum. "I'm sorry that I misunderstood."

"That's okay, sir. I'm learning a lot tonight."

Chichak's face worked to ignore the statement. The other agents stepped away. Nobody spoke.

"Please tell Mr. Van Leer that I'll be available to see him shortly," Chichak said.

Chapter 25

AMBUSH, WELL-BRED – 3:53 A.M.

Chichak let Runyon lead the way towards the library on the third floor. More liquored chit-chat flowed upwards from the second floor.

My feet padded behind them. I was surprised that they didn't hear me and shoo me away.

"Do we have anything coming in from the field?" Runyon asked.

Chichak slowed his pace. "The snow," he said, forcing a chuckle. "They never taught us to plan for a blizzard, did they? All those training sessions at Quantico, but they forgot the blizzard scenario."

Runyon did not answer.

He just kept walking.

That was a trick I used on Patrol. When anger flushed through me, and my chest pounded, I would try to say nothing and walk away. The method saved me from more than a few complaints. Unless I had to stay nailed down there at the scene of commotion where trouble was a-brewin', I learned the value of a getaway.

They were headed for the library.

I broke off down the hallway to the left.

The library had two doors that opened on different sides. The architect had a lot of energy, no doubt because his New Gilded Age client had a lot of money.

I button-hooked around, edged one door open and stayed dead still. Van Leer with Chichak might be worth overhearing.

"Director Chichak, I wanted to speak to you," Van Leer said as he sank into a leather armchair.

Chichak avoided looking at Runyon.

"Mr. Van Leer," Chichak said, "Special Agent Runyon was assigned to liaise with you. Believe me, he is more than capable of handling anything you need."

"Excuse me," Runyon said.

He turned and left the library.

Both men watched him go and then looked back at each other.

"I have to go get back to our Kidnap Squad," Chichak said.

"I'm sure that you're both a father and a husband," Van Leer said. "As such, I need you to hear me out."

If either of them turned, they would see my door open a few inches. I eased it shut to just a crack, but I could still hear and see them.

"In a crisis like this, a man turns to his friends," Van Leer said.

The other door opened. Some guests entered. They had been sitting quietly in the den, or else I would have heard them.

Nine of them squeezed themselves into the library.

Chichak rose from his chair.

"Sir, I can't run a complex capital case like this and take time off for meetings," Chichak said. "I was told that you wanted to speak to me alone."

"That was not my message. Not my understanding at all."

"Come now, Director," said the sweet-faced woman with the shag haircut. "Are we that threatening to a high-ranking FBI officer?"

"No, ma'am." Chichak tried a smile that did not mask his huge annoyance. "But unless we have some new data to warrant this conversation, I really cannot spare the time."

"This deliveryman, this Max," Sweetface said. "The one that you're squiring around. He tried to date Bess a long time ago."

I started. That was false. I had never seen Bess before tonight.

"Tried to date?"" Chichak asked.

"A seduction dinner that never came off, from what I hear," she said.

"This neighborhood always has its share of hustlers and predators," Patrician Eyeglasses said. "They see the naive daughters and try to move right in."

"And these men are often rough-hewn and earthy," Sweetface said. "Very different from the genteel college boys that these girls have dated. They come from different worlds. You know how exciting that can be to a sixteen-year-old."

Someone was fabricating fairy tales about me. Dating Bess Van Leer was something that I could never see myself doing. Boredom would hit me halfway through our first bowl of New England clam chowder together. She would want some ice-cold Vichyssoise, and I would long to gnaw on a Nathan's frank, heavy on the mustard and sauerkraut, from the cart on the corner.

"Where did you hear this dating story?" Chichak asked.

"Do you doubt me?" she said.

"Not at all. I'm just anxious to verify this story as soon as possible."

"I honestly don't remember where I heard it," the woman said.

"Please try," Chichak said.

Her fine-boned face chilled.

"I will," she said. Liquor slurred her words with anger.

She squinted at Chichak, and he looked away.

"I think that you should arrest this Max character," Van Leer said.

"We all do," Sweetface said.

"We are all standing together on that, Mr. Chichak," the man with the Santa Claus pin said. "Except you."

"We – none of us – understand your reluctance," Patrician Eyeglasses said. "And, despite what some may say, we are not dilettantes here. Why, in this very room we have a nationally syndicated columnist and a sitting federal judge."

Chichak scanned them again.

"Don't tell me who," he said. "It's better that I don't know."

He smiled.

Nobody smiled with him.

"Chichak!" I said to myself. "Get out of this library! You can't win. Nobody could."

"Now, we agreed not to use anyone's job as an argument," Van Leer said. "That was a ground rule, I thought."

"If I arrest Max, he gets legal protection," Chichak said. "Much more than he has now. He's the wiseguy type who has to show he can outtalk and outsmart the world."

"Hmm," I thought. "Rather blunt fellow there."

"Keeping him talking makes it all admissible in court," Chichak said. "If I arrest him, he will find a lawyer who will tell him to shut up. And that lead will wither up. So I'm keeping him talking."

"I know why you're being stubborn about this," Santa Claus Pin said. "Earlier in your career, you were stubborn. And the Bureau punished you for it."

"I think I just found our syndicated columnist," Chichak said.

"Read in my next column on the mess you're making here tonight," Santa Claus Pin said, scratching his hand. "And your early troubles in the Bureau."

"I'm afraid my decision stands," Chichak said.

He straightened up even more.

"I'm still the one running this case."

Chapter 26

BREAKING AND ENTERING – 4:27 A.M.

Chichak slumped out of the library scrum as I stayed in my hidey-hole.

The crowd of inquisitors looked quite pleased with themselves. But they had too much breeding to say so.

Giving Chichak time to knit himself back together, I dawdled, and then located him on the stairs to the kitchen.

"My Dad was a printer who never got out of the rat race," I said. "When I was growing up and learning about mean rich kids, I wanted to learn their secret."

"Which is what? And did you?"

"There is no secret. They are just mean."

"Does it matter?"

"I'm afraid that it does. They run everything."

"That's simplistic," he said.

"They don't run you, Chichak. I see that."

His executive eyes hooded over.

"You seem to keep prying where you don't belong."

"I came here to deliver a case of Chateau Unpronounceable."

"So you're forcing yourself to belong?"

"I don't belong anywhere, Chichak. When this is over, prison, morgue or my six-floor walk-up studio apartment, I'll still be out of place."

"There's no time for this."

"There is for this. I overheard some of those blueblood ax-men talk about your meeting just now," I lied.

"Did you?"

"And I admire your courage," I said truthfully.

"And?"

"I'm never going to like you, Chichak. But I admire you. Part of me wishes that I had gone your way."

All of me ached to say that I had recently lived in the underworld of discipline that he was crawling through at the moment. But if I told him that, he might guess that I was an ex-cop.

"Excuse me," he said, the smooth executive again, "but I've got to find Special Agent Runyon."

"You're careful to use his full title now?"

"You do take chances in how you talk to me."

"Don't worry too much about your relationship with Runyon being damaged," I said. "He understands what you meant by 'boy'. It wasn't his generation's problem."

"How would you know?"

"I hate racism and racists. But you're not one. Runyon knows that. So does the Bureau."

∞

My feet dragged heading back up the staircase. I wanted to clutch Francesca and dive into a plush bed with her to sleep like children for days. But, as Chichak kept saying, there was work to do.

Francesca was not in sight. The guests were preparing for an all-nighter until Huggy returned.

Trying for the third floor, my leg muscles kept pushing me upwards. The left side of my chest started to throb from forty-six years of punishment, signs of an old enemy.

The steps welcomed me. I slumped backwards. Then I heard Evers' voice on the landing above me. Her distinctive voice stayed in my brain-box.

"The fact that you are on everyone's radar is your business," she was saying. Her voice was gray neutral.

For a second, I thought Evers was talking to me. But she was speaking to someone else.

"But I need you to square the corners," she continued, "and be more professional. Thank you."

She did not give the other person, obviously another agent, any time to speak or object. The talk was already over.

This was my night for eavesdropping.

To maintain peace in the universe, my body forced itself back down the stairs and into an armchair as befitted my health.

Evers came down the stairs stridently in her white lace evening dress. Diascu, the spanked one, trailed behind her. His milky face was expressionless.

The pair just nodded to me as they passed. The guests in the other rooms were making too much distraction for one to register the tense atmosphere.

☙

Francesca was at the fringe of the crowd in the main living room. The sight of a cigar in her ringed fingers startled me.

"Famous women who puffed cee-gars," I said. "Bonny Parker, Anne Baxter, Hermione Gingold and Mary Read, the pirate. Among others."

"Smoking calms me," she said. "Who was it who said, 'I like to keep a little smoke between me and the world'?"

"Mrs. O'Leary of Chicago?" I said. "I've been desperately seeking you."

"All your life?"

"If not longer."

She smiled and stroked my arm.

"Will I be able to see you after this terrible might?" she asked. "Or will it remind you of too much pain?"

"I'll ask the warden."

"Please."

"Please yourself," I said. "This Sherlock needs his Watson."

Then I told her about the false story about me dating Bess.

"I bet that Christopher, the one they call 'Mad Dog', started that rumor," she said.

"Why?"

"It's the kind of thing that he would do."

"That's a little thin on details there," I said.

"He doesn't have enough to occupy himself."

"He does now. Hand therapy. Weeks of it."

"Because he fell downstairs?"

"Because he led with his right."

She studied me from an angle, waiting for an explanation. None was forthcoming.

"What can I do to help you?" she asked at last.

"Tell me everything that you know about Bess," I said. "The whole hairball. With the hair on it."

"She's nineteen, fairly unhappy, in Sweetbriar College somewhere in Virginia, uses up boyfriends, and has lots of girlfriends."

"She's nineteen and already has a favorite drink?" I said. "Reminds me of me. Please go find her and get her talking. About herself. You're good enough to do it. Very adroit with your conversation."

"Why?"

"Just trust me."

&#x3;

Ten minutes later, I was tiptoeing up the narrow stairs to the fourth floor. Both sisters had their bedrooms there, according to Runyon's crime scene diagram. I had seen him sketch the house and memorized it.

Huggy's bedroom had austerely pink walls and a somber grey carpet. There was a tidily made bed. On her dressing table, a few ceramic horses pranced protectively beside cosmetics geometrically aligned.

Above the bed was an oil painting of her, looking about fourteen. She was wearing Eastern-style riding gear – equestrian helmet, riding slacks and jodhpurs.

Her room told me nothing.

Terrified and shaky, I fumbled out into the hall but nobody saw me.

Bess's room was different. To begin with, her door was locked. That said something.

Apparently, she did not trust her Daddy's millionaire cronies.

My expired NYC employee health card failed to click open her door latch. But I needed to get in there.

In my NYPD non-career, I had only worked Patrol and never Detectives. Tonight was the time that I had to outthink a kidnapper with a sawed-off shotgun before he used it to turn Huggy into jelly.

So I did what I did not want to do. Heights, cold and stupid risks always frightened me.

But tonight was the big night.

I opened Huggy's window. The snow was gentler now but still falling.

The window opened all the way onto a ledge covered with powder snow. Seven feet away, Bess's window tempted me.

My fingers cleaned off all the snow that I could reach. More kept coming down.

"If you think about this much more, you won't do it," I said aloud.

Then I was outside, toeing my way along the ledge.

My left foot slipped. My finger-tips gripped the window frame and tried to hold on. I nearly purged. But I did not fall.

"Despondent ex-cop defenestrates self," I said.

I could just see the headlines in *The Post*.

Inch by snowy inch, I crept to the matching windows. Lucky that she did not lock them. Nobody would expect a prowler to crawl four flights up.

I unlatched one and nearly fell inside, nearly pulling the curtains down with me.

My jaw dropped. I felt overwhelmed looking at a baroque pandemonium of Overage Teenage Clutter.

Clothes, stuffed animals, bedclothes, magazines, scraps of paper, magazines, a suitcase or two.

Guilt that I was committing some sort of domicile rape melted at the sight of the chaos.

The Academy never taught us how to search a debutante's boudoir, especially a slob's. But I did my best.

I still trembled from my human fly escapade. The room freshener Bess used to hide the smell of stale cigarettes covered the odor of my flu sweat and fear sweat.

I eased open various drawers of her dressing table: a hodgepodge of expensive makeup cases, lipsticks, perfumes, wrinkled lingerie.

And in the bottom drawer: sheaves of rubber-banded letters.

I pulled one out.

It was not a love letter.

It was a final payment due letter from a credit card company.

I examined others. From bank loan departments. Collection agencies. They all wanted their cash.

It seemed that Good Sister Bess was maxed out.

She was too young to have these cards anyway. There must be some sneaky way that she had gotten approved. Maybe Big Daddy Van Leer had paved the way.

The bedroom had its own bathroom. This was no cold-water flat with the sisters sharing shower soap and toothpaste. Playpen architecture ruled.

Her bathroom was a pharmacist's showroom of prescription drug bottles.

I picked one up.

It had expired four years ago.

I glanced at others.

Some of the doctor's names were familiar to me from newspapers. These good doctors had been a little too caring towards their patients. Federal judges had dubbed them "writing doctors" because they would write anything if the price was right. Some of them were now practicing medicine in various federal prisons for thirty-five cents a day.

Soon, one of them might be treating me.

Loban, Prozac, Lithium and other drugs indicated that Bess had mood disorder problems.

There was nothing else to get.

I edged towards her front door. There was no way that I was going back the same way.

A key grated in the lock.

A gulp died in my throat. I felt like retching.

She was coming back inside. Maybe she needed some more pills

The windows looked inviting but a bit too final. I hoped she was too drunk to notice the wet spots from the melted snow that had blown in along with me and would just head straight into the bathroom to preen herself in the mirror.

Time for the closet.

I pushed my way into her rack of perfumey dresses and tried to stay still.

My breathing wheezed out of me.

At least I was blessed that my flu was the achy kind and not the sneezey kind.

The bedroom door opened.

Bess rustled inside, and the bedroom blossomed with the fragrance of rum. Maybe she had drunk up all her vodka.

Her hand touched the closet door. I was still pressed up against me. She was going to see me. She had to.

Squeezing my eyes shut felt screwy. But I did it anyway.

The phone rang.

"Don't touch it!" said a voice that I recognized as Mrs. Van Leer's. She sounded drunk. "It could be the kidnapper."

Chapter 27

THE RANSOM DEMAND – 4:53 A.M.

Bess turned and darted out of the room. Her feet thumped down the stairs.

Trying not to breathe, I inserted my finger between the phone cradle and the handset and lifted the handset to my ear.

"Mr. Van Leer," the man's voice said. "Put $600,000 in cash under the Alice-in-Wonderland statue in Central Park. You saw us take your daughter, and you know what we can do."

The man had no accent at all. There would be no easy way to tag him later.

"Excuse me, sir," Van Leer said. "Can't you see that there's a blizzard?"

"Mr. Van Leer, don't bother reading from a script. Have the cash there at midnight. You bring it. Come alone, sir. Don't risk your daughter's life for money that you don't need."

"Sir, you're giving me a task –"

The phone went dead.

ಜ

Trying to move like a cat, I hit my shin on the doorway but I got out of the bedroom.

Feet sounded throughout the house. Guests and agents bumped into each other and then disengaged. A babble of voices sounded.

Francesca came up from the staircase. My chest swelled.

Van Leer came behind her, talking to Runyon.

"Why did they have to kidnap her on Christmas Eve?" Van Leer muttered. "Getting that much cash has been a hell of a problem."

"Were you successful?" Runyon asked.

"Barely," Van Leer grunted.

He was seething. His speech suffered.

"I'll be able to repay the money when the banks open, but it's going to be years before I'm able to repay all the markers I've called in."

Francesca and I drifted closer to the fireplace.

"Van Leer really is the take-charge type," I said. "His own daughter kidnapped at gunpoint, and he starts lining up his assets right away. Cash ready to fly."

"And you admire that?" she asked.

"I suspect it. This could turn out to be an inside job. He could be pocketing cash from family members richer than he."

"You are pretty cynical about this, aren't you?" she asked.

"Nope. Around these types, I'm realistic."

"Bess did not want to speak with me," she said. "I'm going to try again."

She drifted sway, leaving her scent behind for me to savor.

Chapter 28

SETTING UP THE STAKEOUT – 5:17 A.M

"Rover agent teams," Chichak said into a radio set on the desk in Van Leer's study. "Check for any fixed surveillance near the Alice-in-Wonderland statue in the park."

The radio went quiet.

"Sir, just where is that statue?" the voice in the field asked. "Exactly, I mean."

"By the boathouse," Chichak said.

"Sir, let me," Evers said. She leaned her runner's body forward and took the radio mike. "New York 1127, that is just off Fifth Avenue at 75th Street, inside the park. It's a sailboat pond. I brought you all there during Orientation. Do you remember now?"

A painful pause took over the radio.

"Yes, ma'am," the voice said. "We're en route now."

Chichak shook his white-haired head.

"Amazing," he said. "How can a New York agent not know that statue?"

"Go easy on him, sir," Evers said. "He's from Utah."

"Then why doesn't he ask his partner?"

"His partner's from South Dakota."

"Night vision capacity set up from the Parks Department building at the sailboat pond," Chichak said. "SSG called up to blanket the area."

Shorthand for "Special Support Group."

"Try to get some of our taxicabs through the snow and over to them."

Other agents were setting up plans on their cellphones.

"Have the gun vault opened," Chichak went on. "Issue out the H&K MP-5s and the Remington 870s to all teams. Subject is approx 602, weight approx 170, NFD, still is Unsub. Black ski parka jacket, bluejeans, brown hiking boots. Weapon seen is a double-barreled sawed-off shotgun, approx eighteen-inches long, wire loop holding muzzle to the victim's head."

Different screens on the desk showed the area near the Alice statue.

"SOG Washington is watching us work this," Chichak announced to the agents. "And they just sent us some cheery news. Special Agent Lincoln Diascu has just been promoted to Assistant Special Agent in Charge, Honolulu Field Office, effective January One of next year."

The agents cheered and catcalled. Some clapped. Diascu stopped working, head ducked down above the tuxedo shoulders, half-smile teasing his mouth.

"You bypassed ranks to get there!" Runyon said. "No S.S.A. or that jazz. Always said you were a clever guy."

I turned to Evers, who was unrolling a map of Manhattan.

"Why the promotion?" I asked. "Do you have ranks in your Bureau?"

"S.A. Diascu worked on an extremely complex spy case in FCI – Foreign Counter-Intelligence. The case lasted two years and involved three South African nationals. And, yes, we have ranks. S.S.A is one up from Special Agent. Supervisory Special Agent, or S.S.A, is what I am."

"So, up until right now, you outranked Diascu?"

She looked at me coolly.

"I've been in longer," she said.

"Thanks, guys and gals," Diascu said. "We all know that this comes from the Martinraak FCI mess. I only wish that it has been shoot 'em up bank robbery subjects instead of FCI. But I won't forget where I came from."

"After tonight, drinks are on you," Evers said.

"That's right," Diascu said. "Walker's Pub, off Canal Street, as usual."

"This S.A. is stuffing toilet paper in his dress shoes to stay warm in the park," Runyon said, smiling his smile that never reached his eyes. "And I don't care who knows it."

"If you lose your toes to frostbite," Levin said, "the Bureau will issue you some new ones."

"Gentlemen and ladies," Van Leer said. "I'll be going out with you. But I'm a ski bum myself and know how cold the park can be. If you need thermal socks, a down vest or anything, you have only to ask."

"Nossir, we can't," Diascu said. "Regulations."

"But that's absurd."

"Nossir, that's the Bureau."

"Bureau," a few of them echoed.

Teams filed out of the brownstone in muttering clumps.

"Chichak, I want to go with you," I said.

"That's impossible. You're a subject."

"Why not call me 'a suspect'?"

"The Bureau prefers the term 'subject'. As in 'the subject of our investigation'. It's more neutral than the term 'suspect', which sounds somewhat derogatory."

"You have time to discourse on your jargon right now?" I asked.

"You're right. It is not the right time."

"Then if I'm the subject, that makes you the king."

The front doorbell rang.

೮ঙ

Runyon stepped over in his tissue-wadded shoes and opened it.

Two slim executive-types in overcoats stood in the doorway. They held out their FBI credentials in black leather folders.

"S.A.'s Durden and Kicklighter," the taller one announced. Then he mumbled something.

"Good, great," Chichak said. "I'm Deputy Assistant Director Chichak. We can use you to cover the 79th Street Transverse into the park. Did you get the subject description?"

The taller one shook his head. His five o'clock shadow would always emphasize the glint of his wire-rim glasses.

"Sir, I guess that you did not hear us," he said. "We work out of OPR."

"Office of Professional Responsibility," the other one said. He was balding, with blond hair and black eyebrows above a mouth crowded with crooked teeth. "We're here to investigate the alleged racial comment made by you, sir."

"Wait a second," he said. "You're investigating me now? In the middle of a high-risk operation with a life at stake? At five a.m. the morning of Christmas Eve?

"Sir, it could be worse," observed Darden. "It could be Christmas Day."

"This is a retarded conversation that defies all logic," retorted Chichak.

"Logic is one thing, and rules are another," the taller one said. "Rules say that an OPR investigation must commence ASAP."

"Your mother commences ASAP," Diascu said, pulling on his gray topcoat over his tuxedo.

"Excuse me," the taller one said. "I'm S.A. Kicklighter. Who are you, sir?"

"I'm a working brick agent," Diascu said.

He stepped closer.

"Like you used to be," he continued. "Do you know that we've got a victim still at risk in this operation? And why on God's green earth are you starting this case, if you can call it that, at this time of the morning?"

"Expediency, sir."

"Aww, come on," Diascu said. "You're doing this tonight because you happened to be in the neighborhood, figured to score some overtime so you can goof off the rest of the Christmas holidays."

The OPR rats looked at each other.

"And if you're not sure about the name," Diascu said. "I'll make it easy for you. D-I-A-S-C-U. Assistant Special Agent in Charge."

When the rats heard the rank, they wilted just a tad.

"Tomorrow, gentlemen," Diascu said. "Plenty of time for you then. You might want to note that DAD reported himself to you for this violation."

The two OPR types melted from the doorway and back out into the cold.

"That's how to be a boss," I said.

"How would you know?" Chichak asked.

"But I worry about your career, Diascu," I said. "With a few more sweet interviews like that."

Diascu's mouth quirked.

"Bureau," he replied.

"That word is getting a real workout tonight," I said.

ᘓ

Chichack and I stood in the hallway again. Exhaustion and stress pushed me to lean against the wall.

"Chichak, you need to take me along because I saw the suspect up close."

"Subject," he said automatically.

"Okay, then. Subject. I fought with him. I know how he moves and what his body looks like."

"You've already given us a description," Runyon said.

"A description can only take you so far. Wouldn't it strengthen your case in court if I can identify him by his body size and shape in person just a few hours after we fought? I think that it would."

Chichak looked me over for a minute.

Runyon's phone hummed, and he took the call. His face showed emotion for once – he looked worried.

"Sir, you may not want to take Max with you," Runyon said. "That call was about him. I think that we now know all about him."

Chapter 29

BUREAU STORY – 5:28 A.M.

"Max here is Max Royster," Runyon said. "And he used to be an NYPD cop."

My body twitched towards the Van Leer front door.

Chichak's jaw dropped. He stared at me.

"I can't believe that," Chichak said. "I've been in the Bureau since I was a baby agent, twenty-seven years ago, and worked with every kind of police official imaginable. But I cannot imagine him on the Job in any kind of uniform whatsoever, even in the most Podunk backwater two-man department in the country."

"It still surprises me," I said. "Sometimes on rainy Tuesday nights I just lie in bed and giggle to myself."

"Why aren't you an officer at present?" Chichak asked.

"We've got a date in the park, so let's go," I said. "I can spin the tale of my resume on the way there."

"We're not taking my Cadillac," Chichak said.

My wallet still lay under the front seat. Maybe the agent who kept quoting J. Edgar Hoover would find it, steal my identity and become me. It would be many steps down for him on the winding staircase of life.

"And why not?" I asked.

I needed my wallet. It had some free meal coupons at horrible fast food restaurants inside. And other stuff that Chichak could use to doubt me more, like cellphone numbers of some very odd Playpenners.

Chichak looked at me.

"Because I like your Cadillac," I said, to cover up. "It's warm!"

Chichak getting his mitts on my wallet would strengthen his position. He could check more files with the different cards in that wallet.

"Here's why not," he said.

A huge blocky snowplow turned onto the street, pushed towards us through the packed snow and stopped.

"Up we go," Chichak said.

He watched me climb into the snowplow cab beside the driver and then joined us.

The snowplow driver was a heavy-bellied black man chomping a wet cigar above his brush of a goatee.

The cab smelled of beer and dead cigar smoke.

"Where to, dad?" he wheezed.

"East 72nd Street. The entrance to the park," Chichak said. "We'll move real slow until we get there. Our subjects may be watching the whole area."

"You call it, dad," he said.

"What's with this 'dad' routine?" I asked. "Is he the last of the beatniks or something?"

"'Dad' stands for 'Deputy Assistant Director', white-bread," he said. "And just so you know, I'm Special Agent Hubert Cumberbatch, 22 years, Eff-Bee-fucking-Eye, and I don't like jodie civilians in my operation."

Chichak kept talking in his cellphone, checking positions like a stage manager choreographing an epic production.

The streets seemed like long alleys with cream covers over them. Traffic consisted of a single a taxi cruising Park Avenue. Aside from that, the Playpen looked empty of life.

CB

The park was a different story. We came in through the wide traffic entrance on East 72nd Street. Playpenners were out, modeling their ski outfits. Genteel grandmothers walked their poodles in the snow. Maybe they thought that the storm would worsen.

"Look at these nutcases," Special Agent Hubert Cumberbatch said. "Taking advantage of a blizzard so they don't have to hump up to Vermont and pay lift fees. Dogwalkers letting Bowser roll in the goddamn snow. Other idiots speed-walking or trying to jog. Ain't no way I'd ever be out in that mess."

We entered the park and sat in the snowplow cab, waiting.

"Why are you interfering with my case if you're an involved subject?" Chichak asked.

"The eternal question," I said. "As soon as the client with the sawed-off slugged me, I got very involved."

"And so?"

"And so I am pals with the demimonde who hang on in the Playpen. The Playpen spans the East Side, 59th to 96th Street, and besides the Hinwies –"

"The whats?" asked Cumberbatch.

"High Net Worth Individuals," I told him. "There's a whole other world with bartenders, ex-soldiers, sex workers, pro boxers, out-of-work actors, bike messengers, EMS paramedics, off-duty cops, etc. You get the idea. I call them the 'Playpen Irregulars'. Just like Sherlock Holmes had his Baker Street Irregulars. They are scouring the Playpen streets right now, looking for my van."

"I have some difficulty believing that they're doing this without pay on a night like tonight."

"How many close friends do you have, Chichak?"

He did not answer.

"The career, huh?" I asked. "Well, sometimes I've got too many. My lawyer contacted them. They're doing this for me and for Huggy."

"It still seems like a Huck Finn fantasy."

"When you have a missing child, don't you have hundreds of volunteers who risk their lives in the woods, deserts or mountains at night to find him or her? Why should the Irregulars be any different?"

Cumberbatch snorted.

"I don't want to duplicate work," I said. "You put some agents out to hunt my van. How many do you have out there?"

Chichak stayed quiet again.

My breath came out from my mouth in the frigid cab. My body rocked in the tin seat.

"You don't have any out there, do you?" I asked.

Chichak could handle a direct question.

"Not now," he said.

"Did you ever have any teams looking for my van?" I asked.

My voice rose. Cumberbatch threw me a harsh look.

"Priorities," Chichak said.

"Explain that, please."

"Washington thought that the van had left the area, if not the city," Chichak said. "They refused to allocate teams for a fruitless search."

"And you didn't tell me? And you didn't argue with Washington. You're a DAD. What could they do to you?"

"Shut up, you dumb cacknacker," Cumberbatch said. "They could fire him and yank his pension if he disobeyed them. You got no idea what you're talking, whitebread."

"So this is just a show?" I asked.

"If she dies, he lives with that forever," Cumberbatch said. "We all do. You don't, player. I know that you're a local civvy character who is driving everyone crazy. So don't get preachy."

"Royster, why are you no longer an officer?" Chichak asked.

"Depression. And a few other head problems."

"Did you get a pension?"

"Not yet. They're hoping that I give up the fight. In one way or another."

"Then how do you survive?" he asked.

"I spend a lot of time asking myself that same question. Bar-back jobs, moving furniture, driving a gypsy cab, archaeology projects, substitute teaching. Kind of like young Abe Lincoln, but no longer very young."

"That makes you look ripe for a kidnap job," he said. "You need money quite sharply."

Cumberbatch pushed the snowplow onto the East Drive and stopped it. We were now in between the Sailboat Pond and the Rowboat Lake and near the Ramble, a dense wooded section with frozen waterfalls and streams, about a football field away from the bronze Alice-in-Wonderland statue.

"Here's where I get off and leave you gentlemen," Cumberbatch said. "I'll be back in about forty-five minutes."

"Why?"

Cumberbatch blew out a breath, his cheeks puffing.

"Because I'm supposed to be a Civil Servant," he said. "And, as a Heavy Vehicle Operator, this is my meal period. I'll meet the other Operators at the Parks Department shed for coffee and Danish. They don't know that I'm an agent. I been working with them for seven months. If I don't show up, they will wonder why. Maybe they'll call my boss, worried that I might be hurt or dying of a fat man's heart attack. So I go."

With that he switched off the ignition and swung down from the snowplow's cab.

C3

"Chichak, I'm getting colder already. How about if I give you the flu?"

Chichak shivered himself, hunching his shoulders.

"We Bureau veterans traditionally tell stories during stakeouts," Chichak said. "Is that all right with you?"

"Of course," I said. "I'm interested to know how you think."

"Really?"

"And there's no radio," I said.

"The Academy at Quantico took everything out of us," he said. "Tests, tests, tests. *The Code of Hammurabi. The Magna Carta.* Constitutional law. Marbury versus Madison. If you dropped below a B average, the Academy dismissed you in disgrace. Forgive me if I sound elitist. But our Director, Mister Hoover, thought that it was better to teach smart people to become federal agents than it was to teach federal agents to become smart people.

"And the physical training! Running all over the Virginia woods until we thought that we would drop dead. In those days, we had to run a mile and a half in less than twelve minutes, crank out eighty pushups in two minutes, seventy sit-ups in two minutes and do six or more pull-ups. By the time graduation came, we were toughened up and proud to be baby agents of the FBI.

"But right after the graduation ceremony, one of the New Agent Counselors approached my roommate, Blake Yaris, and me. There was a 'Bureau Special' developing in Pennsylvania and they needed more agents. Even if we were brand-new Academy recruits, they wanted us there right now. Blake and I had scored well on the firearms range with the .38 revolver, 12-gauge pump, Thompson sub-machinegun and Remington 30-30 rifle. Those were the primary weapons authorized back then."

"What's a 'Bureau Special'?" I asked.

"A 'Bureau Special' is whenever Washington deems a case to have sufficient importance to warrant extra agents and resources to go there. There is no limit. Now you and your parlor-pink buddies like that liquor store owner –"

"Mr. Tash?"

"– may guffaw over your joints of Panama Red about us. But when the Bureau decides that a case is a 'special', we are truly unstoppable."

"What was this Pennsylvania thing?" I asked.

"Kidnap."

We both let that hang.

"I don't suppose that anyone ever threatened to kidnap you, Royster."

"They know that the most ransom money my family could raise would be about a nickel ninety-eight."

"So most citizens never even think about what it would be like to be chained, starved, dumped in a hole, wondering if anyone is looking for you, if they've given up, if they're goofing off and just going through the motions of searching for you. When I am assigned to case, I do not just go through the motions."

"I see that."

He shivered and drew his camel-hair coat even tighter.

"Any chance we could turn the heater on?" I asked. "I'm not used to the cold."

We both studied the snowplow console. Hubert Cumberbatch had taken the keys with him.

Chichack shrugged and drew his coat even tighter around himself.

"Blake and I sped away from the graduation party, with all the Bureau families and their kids and the speeches and the drinks. We crossed over the state line and kept going. There were no airports near the site, so driving was the fastest way to get there.

"We got off the Turnpike and took roads that got smaller and smaller. Fewer farmhouses by the roadside. Thick woods surrounded us. They blotted out the moonlight. We were going back in time, leaving the Quantico Academy far, far behind us.

"For years, the people around there, a hamlet called Shade Gap, Pennsylvania, had been living in fear. A mysterious man with a high-powered hunting rifle had been attacking them for no reason. Some had seen him up close. He never spoke. He would appear on the edge of a clearing at sundown and shoot at the locals. One man took a slug in the leg so badly that they had to amputate it. He did his farm chores on crutches afterwards.

"This was the kind of country place where locals seldom ever moved away. They were born there, went to high school, married and raised families. Everyone hunted for food. Each house had shotguns and rifles. They carried them openly. But one of them was this sniper. They called him the 'Mountain Man'.

"The Pennsylvania State Police, a strict, military operation, could do nothing. They had no way to hunt this Mountain Man. At this time, they had no profilers, no one delving into the mind. They'd originally been formed in 1900 or something to protect the mining interests in the Commonwealth of Pennsylvania. Their title had been 'The Coal and Iron Police'. People called them a kind of horse cavalry, with snappy uniforms perfect for parades but not very well suited for modern fact-finding. They just told locals to be on the alert at sundown, not go outside and keep their doors locked.

"The Mountain Man shot and wounded others, right near their houses. Nobody was safe, no matter what they did.

"One evening, wearing a mask, he sprang from the woods and grabbed a woman who was doing chores. He tried pulling her into the woods. She knew that he would kill her in those woods. She fought like a tiger, and he had to keep hold of his rifle with one hand and control her with the other. She broke free, screaming for her husband. The Mountain Man vanished back into those woods without saying a word.

"Earlier that morning, while Blake and I had been checking our business suits for the day's graduation ceremony, a 16-year-old girl, Peggy Ann, was waiting for the school bus with her sisters. The Mountain Man suddenly appeared, menaced them with a shotgun, then seized Peggy Ann and pulled her into the woods."

"The girls screamed, 'The Mountain Man's got Peggy Ann!' Nobody heard them. He pulled her deeper into these same woods till they completely concealed the pair. They covered them up. This was an area where they could live for years and nobody would see them.

"As soon as the villagers heard, the men armed themselves and raced into the woods. Everyone helped. They knew the land from hunting it and how lonely it was. Mountain lions, timber rattlers and wild boar roamed free in it. Some hunters never came home. Nobody ever knew what happened to them.

"The Bureau's Harrisburg Field Office was notified. But that was more than fifty miles away. We had nobody closer. Agents raced to the scene and set up a command post like we did tonight.

"Blake and I got to the command post that night and reported in. Nobody cared that we had just been sworn in. They knew that a young girl's life hung in the balance. If he got her away from our search parties and into the mountains, we would never find him. She would be his sex slave for life.

"These same woods scared Blake and me, but of course, we didn't say so. We were young and tough and we were the FBI.

"A veteran agent named Terry joshed us about being rookies and showed us the tent where we would be sleeping. Other agents slept on the ground or in their cars. We were all strongly committed, just like you saw tonight. That Evers, in her flimsy party dress and coat, standing post outside in a snowstorm and refusing a replacement."

"While she was doing it, no doubt she was reciting the mantra, 'Bureau'," I said.

Chichack was annoyed by both the interruption and its tone, but that was all right with me. The cab could use all the heat it could get.

"That's all that she would have to say," snapped Chichak. "Shots were fired all night. Some volunteers were shooting at anything. We could not persuade them to stand down. As you said before, the kidnapper often kills an adult victim to have no witnesses. Our subject was heading for a ridge of wilder mountains where an army of us could never find him. If he got past us to that ridge, the victim was finished. So we were racing against time.

"A local hunter named Bilwig knew all the land here. Not many others did. Bilwig was one of the few who had hunted everywhere within a fifteen-mile radius. He was sharp, friendly, in good physical shape and gave us a dozen good reasons why he should guide us. But the Bureau frowns on using volunteers to track an armed suspect. Especially with an innocent victim."

"Like tonight," I said.

"Correct. So we put Mr. Bilwig off. Too many things could go wrong. We told him, 'Not right now.' He took the rejection easygoing. I told you that he was smart.

"That night, the wind blew cold through our tent all night. It was still late winter there in March. Blake and I shivered under our blankets."

"Was it as cold as tonight?"

"Colder. And there wasn't any alcohol before we went out. We thought about our Academy classmates lying with their wives in bed, stuffed after the celebration dinner, with a week off to report to their new duty stations. Our new .38 Smith & Wesson revolvers lay in our holsters next to us. We hoped that tomorrow we would acquit ourselves in the highest tradition of the Bureau. But we were scared about what might go wrong.

"The next day, we suited up for the search. Bilwig was up with us and waiting to lead our team into the woods. Troopers and agents mixed into our team. We were still unsure about letting Bilwig lead or not. The agent in charge, I forget his name, but I will always remember his face, asked for a show of hands. It was five of us for letting him lead and five against. That was no good. A tie vote would not help us. So the agent called for a second vote. This time, I changed my vote. I voted to let Bilwig lead. I don't know why. Maybe because two of the troopers voted for Bilwig to lead and three of the agents did. I thought that he could do a good job for us.

"Despite our public relations, not all agents are in top physical shape. Some work wiretaps on their fannies, some just refuse to exercise, and others are prone to gain weight easily. But Blake and I were in top physical shape. So they put us in the front line of searchers going through pine and oak groves looking for any sign of the subject.

"Bilwig kept leading us, going through the thick woods. He was doing well. We avoided swamps that left other agents muddy and exhausted. He knew how to make good time.

"After three or four hours of this, we were bone-weary. But Bilwig was not. 'Don't you want to stop this creature?' he kept asking us. 'Come on, come on. Let's go.'"

"With Bilwig leading, we were ahead of the other search groups. Way ahead. And we liked that. Blake and I were still thinking like Academy recruits. Compete, compete, compete. The others worked to keep up with us. They were starting to tire, but we were still fresh. And, like all youngsters, we wanted to show it off a bit. It was just harmless, you know. The kind of thing that, later on, agents learn not to do. But we were just baby agents.

"The others were dragging their tails behind us. But we were going to get Peggy Ann and nothing was going to stop us.

"The air was still sharp and fresh, hunter's air. We were going to end this two-year reign of terror.

"We slogged up a hill. A small white dog came barking like crazy towards us. We asked Bilwig about it. Bilwig said that it was just a stray dog. It didn't look like any stray to me. He was too well cared for. I should have said something. But I was a new baby agent and did not want the veterans thinking that I was a worrier.

"We found out later that everyone knew that the dog belonged to a loner, a strange recluse named William Diller Hollenbaugh. He and the dog always stayed together. It was his only contact. Everyone knew that. The few people who knew Hollenbaugh figured that he might be the Mountain Man. Bilwig knew about Hollenbaugh and his dog. But he was too excited to tell us, right there. Or maybe he had tunnel vision at that moment. We never knew.

"The dog kept barking.

"Hold it!" one of the troopers said. "'We're too far ahead of the others.' The brush was so thick that we could not see thirty feet ahead of us. It screened everything from us. Just then, we saw Peggy Ann. She screamed, 'He's going to kill me!'

"Hollenbaugh rose up next to her and fired his shotgun. The agent named Terry spun around and went down, blood everywhere. Two agents fired their .38s. But the girl and Hollenbaugh had melted back in the woods.

"I ran to Terry and tried to give him first aid, like they had trained us at the Academy. But it was no use. He wheezed in once, and then his face froze. He died while I was looking at him, trying to stabilize him."

"Hundreds more agents flew in after Terry died. They found Hollenbaugh the next day. He was SWRA."

"Slain-While-Resisting-Arrest?" I dredged the initials from somewhere deep in my packrat memory.

Chichak nodded.

"Peggy Ann was saved. The President spoke and praised Terry's courage. The Bureau held inquiries, interrogated me, Bilwig and everyone else in our group. Bilwig was a fast-talking friendly kind of guy with a quick wit. Kind of like you, Max. That's when I swore never to trust an outsider, a stranger, even a local cop, on any dangerous Bureau task."

The cold skewered me.

"How do you guys stand this temperature?" I asked. "Don't tell me. I know. Bureau."

That did not sweeten the atmosphere.

A fine mist of snow had accumulated on the windows and windshield, turning the snow-white world outside soft-focus.

Chapter 30

ROLLING THE DICE – 5:56 A.M.

Cumberbatch swung himself back up into the snowplow cab.

"Damn, it's cold in here," he said. "Why didn't you switch on the heater?"

"Because you took the keys with you," said Chichack.

"Oh, yeah," said Cumberbatch, seemingly genuinely surprised. He would go far in the Bureau.

He slid the keys into the ignition and turned on the heater.

To me, the air coming out didn't seem much warmer than the air outside, but it seemed to satisfy Cumberbatch.

Suddenly, the radio crackled to life.

"Victim's father is now entering the park on foot from East Seven-Two Street," the radio said.

Chichak took a heavy breath and picked up the radio mike.

From my perch, I could look down and see in the lamplight the twelve-foot high statue of Alice and her pals.

Van Leer came into sight, carrying a gray suitcase. He trudged through the fresh snow about forty feet from us.

"The suitcase has a homing device built into the handle," Chichak said. "Plus a bank robbery dye pack and tear gas near the money. We can trigger them by remote, if we need to. The subjects would have to tear apart the suitcase to locate the devices."

We waited some more.

A woman walking a chocolate Labrador strolled in front of us in the semi darkness. A moment later a couple with a cocker spaniel paused nearby. The two canines sniffed each other's crotches with happy tail wags.

"Special Support Group stakeout pair, with the small dog," Cumberbatch said. "I did in-service training with them."

Van Leer left the Drive and slogged through the snow to the statue. When he left, his hands were empty. He had left the suitcase under the statue, as ordered.

"All units," the radio said. "The suitcase is in place."

"Central Park CP, roger," Chichak said.

≪

Minutes dragged.

Then they dragged some more.

"All units," the radio said. "We've got a possible subject on skis approaching. Wearing loose down jacket, possibly green in color."

"Repeat your signal," another radio said. "You're coming in broken up."

Chichak cussed.

"Possible subject approaching on skies," the first voice said.

"Unit, repeat your message," the second voice said.

"Stay off the radio," a third voice said. "Just play it by ear."

"Units, subject is skiing fast now. Be advised that we cannot catch him if he takes the suitcase and speeds up."

"All units, wait for my word," Chichak said. "He cannot ski fast with a suitcase in one hand."

"Visual on subject," another voice said. "Possible subject is a white male, approx six feet, about one-ninety pounds. Green parka and backpack. He could fill that backpack with cash and leave the suitcase and get away."

"That changes things," Cumberbatch said.

The man on skis pushed into our sight. He coasted down the hill towards the statue and vanished.

"Unit, repeat."

"Stand by."

"Is that the subject?"

"He is stopping by the sailboat pond now," a voice said. "About six meters from the suitcase."

"Is he picking it up?"

"Everyone stand down," Chichak said.

"Go for it!" another voice said.

"Does he have it?"

"Take him down!"

"No!" Chichak shouted. "Not until subject is ident."

"He's running!"

From out of nowhere, dark forms raced towards the statue.

Cumberbatch hit the area with a spotlight.

Flares streaked to the sky and burst.

Night turned into day. Cars roared up. Agents in dark blue windbreakers stenciled with the yellow FBI initials poured out of them.

A taxicab jumped the park sidewalk, and Runyon leaped out. He pointed an assault rifle towards the statue.

The dogwalkers flashed past on foot, running from this scene.

More spotlights lit up.

"FBI!" a loudspeaker said. "Freeze!"

"Watch his hands!"

"They've got him!" Cumberbatch said.

"He's moving!"

The same skier lifted up his arms. His hands only held ski poles.

A wave of agents surrounded him.

"Don't move!"

Shotguns waved.

The skier dropped into the snow. Agents with guns pointed at him moved up crabwise, handcuffed him and pulled him to his feet.

The remaining bystanders stood watching.

Diascu holstered his gun.

Other passersby gathered on the Drive near us.

"What the hell happened?" Chichak shouted. "Did he touch the suitcase? Play the video."

"Video rolling now," a deep Midwestern voice said.

"What a mess," Chichak said under his breath.

"Any weapon on him?"

"Negative."

"Any ID?"

Everyone waited.

"He lives three blocks away. No wants or warrants."

Chichak cussed again, so low that I could not hear it.

"Negative, boss," the Midwestern voice said. "He never got within ten feet of the suitcase."

"Goddamnit," Cumberbatch said. "Of all the screwed-up stuff they trained us not to do."

I leaned against the cab door, hanging on. Even through the leather of my jacket I could feel the chill of the handle.

"Any S.A. with a visual see him touch it?" Chichak asked.

That took a while.

"Negative, sir."

"Not on my team."

"Nossir."

"Keep it consensual while we check him through the indices," Chichak said. "Take me to the victim's father."

A dark blue Chevy pulled up next to the snowplow.

Chichak and I hopped down and got inside.

The outside air actually felt warmer than that in the snowplow cab. We both got into the car. I breathed in the welcome heat and Chichak's anger.

∞

The driver brought us to Park Avenue where another van was parked. We reluctantly exited the Chevy and entered the back of a van. Agents with beards and bluejeans were crowded inside.

Van Leer sat on a seat, head in his hands.

"Doorman verifies that subject always skis during storms," the radio voice. "He refuses to come with us to NYFO. Request orders, sir."

"Interview him voluntarily in his residence," Chichak said. "You know how to apologize. If not, learn now."

The radio crackled again.

"In the Hoover days," a voice said. "Nobody made mistakes like we did tonight."

"That's the same nut again," an agent said. "'Special Agent Crackup' is what we're calling him now."

"Cracked up beyond belief."

It was the same agent who had called in the raid on the empty brownstone.

"Training was real back then," the Crackup said. "We knew that we would be facing the worst in the world once we graduated Quantico. Everything is too soft now."

Van Leer's cellphone buzzed. He tried to take it out but could not. An agent reached in and switched it to speaker.

"Yes?" Chichak croaked.

"I saw the whole show," the same voice said. "FBI, huh? All for money, Van Leer. You just killed your little girl."

Chapter 31

MORE ARRESTING CHIT-CHAT 6:43 A.M.

"Ms. Van Leer, I'm Special Agent Evers, and this is Special Agent Diascu," Evers said back at the brownstone. "Is there someplace where we can speak?"

"Not now," Bess said. She smelled of liquor; her voice slurred from it.

"Now would be the best time, miss," Evers said.

Bess looked past them and shook her head. She focused on me and squinted. A full martini glass bobbled in her hand. Her eyes looked like red roadmaps.

"Not tonight," she said. "I'm way too upset. I would not be valuable."

"Listen up," Diascu said. He was playing it harder. "The human memory loses details as time passes. Our studies show that interviews must be done as soon as possible. In fact, I don't know why we didn't speak with you before."

"Some of you tried," Bess said. "But I said no. If you'll excuse me, I feel terrible. I'm going to bed."

She passed by them and went to the doorway.

I got in her way.

"How much do you care about Huggy?" I asked.

"Leave me alone. I don't have to talk to you. You're not the FBI. You're just some kind of phony."

"But I'm a real phony," I said. "My question remains. Why are you not helping us?"

"Daddy!" she shouted.

"He's outside," Chichak said. "Royster, stop this nonsense. Leave her alone. That's an order."

"And I'm a civilian," I said. "I spit in the milk of your orders."

Runyon's grip felt like all his fingers were thumbscrews. I let him walk me away from Bess.

"Her bedroom is on the fourth floor," I said. "But she's heading back to the booze. A little nightcap of Old Stump Remover."

"She's entitled," Runyon said. "Washington wants the boss to arrest you. I haven't told him yet."

"So I don't have much time?"

"I doubt it."

"Runyon, old pal," I said. "How did you ID me?"

He smiled a bit.

"Fingerprints off your cocktail glass. I faxed them to our Ident section and told them it was a special."

"Very tricky," I said. "You should join the FBI."

⅓

Retreating with a bit of dignity into the living room, I saw Francesca sitting by herself, drinking white wine.

"I need your help now," I said.

"What now?" she asked.

"I tried again with Bess. She feels quite unwell."

"She needs help."

"Cue the organ. I need you to witness me taking on Something Big."

She gave me the up-from-under look.

"What do you call 'Something Big'?" she asked.

"The FBI."

"The FBI!"

"Don't worry. You have a very sharp, good mind and you can outthink them. They are civil servants. Nothing more. Just like the Post Office with guns and better clothes."

"Well, I'm not going to do it. They could make my business an absolute hell. Women executives are vulnerable enough."

"Do you feel persecuted?" I asked. "Maybe you should seek professional help."

"Don't try your winning ways on me. I'm refusing."

It took a long time talking to convince her. I did not think that I would. Dragging in her responsibility to the public, her code of ethics, Bunker Hill and the Dewey Decimal System, I finally talked her around to it.

∽

Downstairs, Chichak was sitting by his laptop, talking to Diascu. I inserted myself between them, interrupting their chat.

"What now, Royster?" Chichak asked.

Francesca came past us and stopped. If they turned their heads, they would see her.

"Mad Dog called me from the hospital ER," I lied. "He apologized to me. We're meeting at Legal Aid tomorrow. I found a way to get some cash without working."

Chichak's white eyebrows clashed together.

"For what?" he asked.

"For a lawsuit," I said, still lying. "I'm old friends with the head of Manhattan Legal Aid. If I asked him to, he would sell his wife. And he hates the FBI."

"Sue and be damned to you," Chichak said. "Losers like you try suing the Bureau all the time. They learn."

"Did you think that Mad Dog Christopher would beat me and then not talk about it?"

"What? The question is asinine."

"He's a weepy drunk right now," I said. "Just why did you do it?"

"You needed to tone down a bit," Diascu said.

"So you helped him?" I asked.

Francesca's mouth opened.

"That's enough, Diascu," Chichak said.

"Maybe I should sue more people," I said. "Like ones who just got promoted to Honolulu."

"Don't try it, Royster," Chichak said. "I made that call to soften you up. So would you, in my position. What's more important? A drifter like you getting bruised or Huggy dying?"

Diascu turned and saw Francesca standing within earshot. He touched Chichak's shoulder.

Chichak turned and his eyes widened, seeing Francesca. He sprang out of the chair, spun me around and jammed handcuffs onto my wrists. My aching flu body screamed.

"Enough is enough, Royster," he said. "You've tried my patience once too often."

Chapter 32

BETRAYED BY KISSING – 7:18 A.M.

The handcuffs bit into the tender skin inside my wrists.

"Francesca," I said, the flu and stress cracking my voice. "Call my lawyer Simon Keller. He's listed."

"I can't."

Shock shook my head.

"What?" I asked.

"Francesca Quilloy," she said. "I'm an FBI agent."

She reached into a slit pocket on her hip and showed me a black folder. The same blue-green words "FBI Special Agent" leaped off the card at me. Chichak carried the same creds.

"I betrayed you, Max," she said.

Her voice caught.

"You grabbed me and kissed me," she lied. "I made no move towards you. If I kissed you first, my court testimony would be worthless."

"We both know what happened," I said.

Someone pounded the front door. The doorbell rang.

"EMS!" a man shouted outside the door. "Emergency heart attack call here! Open up!"

"Someone's ill upstairs?" Runyon asked. "I didn't know."

"Come on, open up!" the same man kept saying. "It could be one of yours."

"Open it," Chichak said.

A freckle-faced Irisher in a dark blue Paramedic's uniform bellied inside. Thick glasses magnified his baby-blue eyes. He hoisted an AED Defibrillator against his beer gut.

When I saw him, my body relaxed.

"Heart attack call!" he hollered in a growly Brooklyn accent. "Right here. That's what I told that FBI cub scout blocking off the street out there."

His partner was a tall black woman, hair tied back in a pony tail that emphasized the delicate planes of her face. She could have been a runway model. The agents ogled her and dreamed dreams.

"Lt. Pat Murray, Paramedic," the Irisher said. "Who's running this outfit here?"

"Chichak, FBI."

"Well, Cheech, there's no heart attack call here," Murray the Irisher said. "I just said that to get past your roadblocker. I'm a buddy of Max here."

"One of those Regulars?" Chichak asked.

"IR-Regulars, please," Murray said. "We saw Max's van, the van that you want moving past 63rd Street and First Avenue."

I spun towards them, handcuffs clicking.

"Do you expect me to go running over there?" Chichak asked. "All agents are out checking other leads. There's just a few of us left here."

"Nossir," Murray said. "I don't expect that. I'm good and goddamn mad and pissed off to say that we went into a skid, tapped a tree and lost sight of the van. We looked everywhere then decided to come tell you here."

My leg muscles pushed me over to him.

"Just how the hell did you lose it, Murray?" I asked. "There's a kidnapped teenager inside."

"Why not call the FBI Field Office with this info?" Chichak asked.

"Because you got Max here. Do you think some night-time switchboard operator is going to believe me? Maxy knows me. Right, Maxy?"

"Right, Murray."

"Just how do you know it's the same van?" Chichak asked. "It's covered in snow, isn't it?"

"From the description and the dents and the bumper stickers. You can still see them."

"Sit down," Chichak said. "I'll be right back."

He went into the kitchen. The agents kept looking at Murray's female partner. She smiled and did not say a word.

Chichak's voice rose, arguing.

That was a good sign.

He was probably raising hell with Washington.

He came back out from the kitchen.

"Goddamn Washington," he said. "Royster, they want you arrested for accessory to kidnapping."

I whipped my head back and forth.

"My tax dollars at work," I said.

"You're a bunch of dry-ass sissies," Murray said. "I always thought so. Now I know."

"And you two paramedics are under arrest for Obstructing a Federal Investigation," Chichak said. "Runyon, take them into custody."

I body-blocked Runyon and slammed him back against the wall. He hit the wall and dropped.

"Yow!" Runyon shouted. "I'll kill you!"

Diascu leaped at me. I faked him out, dodged around him and was pounding up the stairs, my hands still cuffed behind me.

"FBI! Freeze!" Diascu shouted.

Francesca tried to run up the stairs. Her tight skirt slowed her down.

The guests came out of the living room. They stared at me.

I kept running.

My chest hurt worse.

○3

On the fourth floor, I saw Bess's door. I reared back, lifted a foot and KICKED as hard as I could.

The door went in a few inches and sagged.

Bess screamed.

— 209 —

I pushed the door open wider, wedged myself inside and grabbed a dresser with my hands behind me.

Using my right hip, I slid the dresser against the door and reinforced it with a heavy armchair.

Someone kicked hard.

The door did not budge.

"Royster, open this door, or we will blast it open!" Diascu shouted.

"Aw, raspberries," I said.

"What do you want?" Bess shouted. More booze smells wafted from her. She was way drunk and sagged to the side.

Reaching down until I thought my shoulders would crack, I stepped backwards and slipped the cuffs around in front of me.

Reaching for my key ring in my front pocket, I juggled out my apartment keys. One was hammered flat, with a pointed edge.

Pointing the edge into the handcuff key well, I pushed hard. Nothing moved.

I tried again.

The same nothing happened.

Then I pushed it in deeper.

Still nothing happened.

My hands shook too much to work the key.

"Royster, this is stupid of you!" Runyon's voice came through the door. "Give it up and I promise you no time in jail. I'll get you treatment."

"What do you want?" Bess asked.

"The truth," I said.

"Daddy!" she wailed.

"Not anymore," I said. "Daddy's gone. He went to find the kidnapper. And you and I are going to talk."

Chapter 33

TELL MR. HOOVER – 7:27 A.M.

"You can't touch me!" Bess shouted.

She sat up in bed, wearing a shortie nightgown.

She was staggering drunk.

"I don't have to," I said "The kidnapper used a shovel in the garden to look normal, shovel snow and blend in. You lied to me. You said that he came in the front door."

"I got confused! You're no detective or anyone that I have to talk to."

"Your DNA was on the shovel," I lied.

"That doesn't prove anything."

"And we've got a good description of him, from your guests. Bartenders and neighbors saw you together. It's all come together."

She swung at me.

I took the punch. But she was too slow to snap it back. My handcuffed arms wrapped around her arm, levered against the elbow and slammed her down onto the floor.

"Royster, give this nonsense up!" Chichak shouted from outside the door.

Kicks banged against the door. The panel sagged. But the dresser wedged the door shut.

We lay in a tangle of limbs on the floor. I had her arm-locked, and we both knew it.

"It's over, Bess," I said, winging it. "You're jealous of Huggy. She's pretty and slim and dresses well. And you talked about it in bars. To anyone who would listen. Falling down drunk. But you never thought that he would do it. Right? It was just bar-talk. Griping about the world."

She tried to get away. Despite the handcuffs, my arms had her locked in.

The door inched open wider. Someone was halfway inside Bess' bedroom.

"He is a hustler type," I went on. "But not a real criminal.

He planned to grab Huggy and escape through your front door. But Huggy fought back. She slowed him down. And he ran into me."

"Let me up!"

"What do you want? You want Huggy back. Tell me where she is. I can't arrest him or you or anyone. I'm a delivery-man. But I can get her back. Without any cops or anything like that. And that's what you really want, isn't it?"

She cried underneath me. I could feel her body vibrate.

Someone squeezed in the front door.

"Bess, I'm your only friend here," I said. "Tell me, and I get her back and everyone's happy."

"He won't let you," she said.

"If I show up at my van, it is all over," I said. "No ransom money. He'll be lucky to just get away and start a new life. I'll explain that to him. I know that I can do it. He releases Huggy, leaves and nobody much cares anymore."

She whipped her head back and forth.

"Tell me," I said. "And I keep you out of it. Huggy will never know."

"79th and East End Avenue," she said. "He's going to bring Huggy to his home in Jersey City. Then he'll try for the money again."

My flu body sagged. Breath came out.

"Okay, you did it," I whispered. "It's over."

"I heard it, too," Diascu said.

He stood halfway inside the doorway, against the dresser I had wedged there.

He stood with his body bladed, like they had trained him to do to protect himself. His hand held the Glock rock-steady and pointed at me. Fear froze me. I was a second away from death. This was way too crazy now. His eyes blazed behind the glasses. He looked me up and down and then at Bess' face. Then the storm passed. He sighed and holstered his gun.

"Don't move, Royster," he said. "You did what no agent could do, breaking in like this. You're cleared now."

My whole body eased and rolled off Bess. I lay on the floor, belly heaving. In my life, I had never been this tired.

"You did it, Max," Diascu said. "Against all odds. You beat us professionals at our game. We in the Bureau all thank you. The guests want you arrested. To keep them happy and to protect Chichak, you'll wear the handcuffs for a bit."

I nodded.

He took out his throat mike and spoke into it.

"This is S.A. Diascu," he said. "The van, victim and subject are at East 79th Street and East End Avenue...Yessir. I'm bringing Royster down now."

Diascu listened to his earpiece. I could not hear anything. He smiled his half-smile.

"DAD Chichak makes just one request, Royster," he said. "When I bring you downstairs and to the Field Office for a statement, he wants you to say something."

"What's that?"

"Nothing," he said, smiling like a farm kid. "Absolutely nothing. He said that he's had enough of you and your talk."

"Deal," I said.

"Not a word."

"You lied to me!" Bess said. "You said that you wouldn't tell anyone!"

"I didn't," I said. "You did. He happened to overhear."

"Ms. Van Leer, I can help you avoid trouble on this," Diascu said. "Go back to sleep and we'll speak in the morning. I think that I can promise you that the Bureau will keep your secret."

Too drunk to snarl no matter how much she wanted to, Bess dragged herself back onto the bed.

ᙕ

Diascu brought me downstairs to the front door. Chichak, Runyon and the team glared at me but said nothing.

Outside, the snow was still coming down. Diascu led me to his car, a black Ford that looked government issue.

I settled into the front seat and put my head back to sleep. My eyes shuttered.

We drove.

He stopped the car.

I looked ahead.

We were at 79th Street and East End Avenue, near the East River. My van was parked there, next to a snow-covered construction sign. I jolted backwards, seeing it.

The FDR Drive was empty of traffic for once. Plastic cones jutted up incongruously orange through the snowplowed drifts. Chunks of gray ice bobbed in the East River.

"Does Chichak have teams already watching it?" I asked. "And he wants me to see the arrest?"

"He doesn't. I do."

"How come you guys don't take this van down right away?" I asked. "Huggy's still in there."

"Mr. Hoover always said that the strength and the reputation of the whole Bureau comes down to one man."

Diascu's voice and rhythm had changed. I turned with the handcuffs clicking.

"You're the Crackup!" I said. "You've been broadcasting all night."

He looked away from me, towards the van.

"And I'm the Special Agent who is going to rescue Huggy and get back some of the Bureau's lost glory," he said.

"No back-up. When you heard me tell DAD Chichak about this location, you thought that my radio was on. It was switched off. They don't know."

"Don't do this crazy thing!" I said.

My voice croaked. I felt like throwing up.

"Huggy could get killed," I said.

"The Bureau has lost so much prestige and rep lately. Too much talking."

He vaulted out of the car and started running towards the van. I jumped out after him.

My feet slid in the snow.

He was charging the front of the van. I pushed myself. I caught up and tried to grab him with my handcuffed hands.

The van rocked. The engine came on. They had seen us.

The van lurched forward, towards the FDR Drive along the river.

"FBI!" Diascu shouted. "Freeze!"

The driver leaned out of the window, driving one-handed. The sawed-off shotgun came up.

Diascu drew and fired. The Glock bucked in his hand.

The windshield cracked.

The van spun.

The shotgun pointed at me. Diascu was two feet from me. He jumped on me, covering my body with his. I went down under him.

The shotgun exploded. I felt the charge hit Diascu. Something stung my legs. Diascu writhed.

"Huggy Van Leer!" he shouted. "This is the FBI! You're safe now."

He rolled on top of me and pointed the Glock at the van. He fired again and again. His hand steadied. He triggered another shot.

The van slowed.

"Tell Mister Hoover I did my best," he said.

Blood covered his mouth and cheeks. It ran from his ear.

The van was lurching onto the Drive.

I scooped up the Glock from his hand and shot three times without aiming from my front-cuffed hands.

The van smashed into a construction fence and crossed to the other side.

It was approaching the river.

The van kept going. It dragged the construction fence with it.

I ran onto the Drive. The East River rippled freezing and uninviting twenty feet away.

The van was inching along.

I ran to the front. The same man who had attacked me less than twelve hours earlier, nylon stocking still pulled down over his face, sagged behind the wheel. I brought up the Glock. It clicked empty. I could not even hurl it at him. I dropped it to the pavement.

He aimed the van at me. I jumped high, hoisted by the bumper. I tumbled with all my momentum and crashed through the cracked windshield. It shattered into nothing as I fell against him.

Gouts of blood splashed from him. Arterial spray stung my eyes as I tumbled into the passenger's seat. He smelled of gun smoke and sweat and dirt.

I got a leg free. It kicked his jaw.

His head whipped back. I pushed myself off of the door and hit him with the handcuffs.

"Help me!" a girl's voice shrieked from the back of the van. "He's going to kill me!"

The van broke through the guardrail of the river. We went in.

Icy water hit. I pulled myself up and rolled into the back.

Huggy thrashed in her red dress. Plastic lock ties held her wrists.

The van spun around in the freezing water.

She clung to me, whimpering a mix of "Help me-Please-Thank you-Oh, God."

"Hold on, but I'm gonna need my hands."

I grabbed her under the arm with my cuffed hands.

The van started sinking.

The front pointed up.

"Hang on!" I shouted.

Huge air bubbles burst upward.

I dragged her forward, over his body and through the empty windshield frame. Metal scraped my face. I kept kicking the water.

"Kick!" I shouted. "Get us clear!"

The van kept sinking.

Gray-black scummy water covered us. Chunks of ice scratched into us. My two hands hooked her left arm and kept gripping. My legs pumped with every last bit of strength I had to propel us upward.

At last we broke the surface, through a kaleidoscope of ice chunks.

I pulled her onto my chest, lay on my back and fought to reach the Drive.

"Don't quit on me!" I hollered. "Or we both drown!"

My fingers were so numb they felt like paws.

We both kicked as we thrashed towards the Drive.

Something hit near us. I grabbed it with both numb hands. It was a cable wire.

Huggy reached for it.

"Just hold on to me."

The wire pulled us towards the Drive.

NYPD cars spun cherry lights over us. Three cops dragged us closer with the wire. Another leaned down and reached for us.

"Take her first!" I shouted. "I'm on the Job!"

"We know, pal," a fat black cop said.

Chichak and Runyon were helping the other cops pull us in. He reached over and dragged Huggy out of the water. She seemed very happy to let go of me.

She babbled, calling for her Mommy and Bess. Words flew out of her.

"Are you all right?" I asked.

"I'm cold, cold, cold," she said.

"We all are tonight," I replied.

The second cop quickly wrapped a metallic survival blanket around her.

Chichak leaned down, his tuxedo snowy and wet. He gripped my forearm and pulled me onto the concrete. I lay there, panting.

"You grabbed the wire from the construction stuff," I panted. "That's probably unauthorized."

"Probably," muttered the third cop, who had a pouchy face and spurred sideburns. He was hovering over me as he ripped open a packet containing a survival blanket. "Now just shut up so I can save your life."

In the background I could see Levin and Gancy and an NYPD cop kneeling by Diascu's lifeless body. Levin was removing his own overcoat and laying it over Diascu's face.

The cop freed my frozen wrists from the cuffs.

ᘓ

"Diascu was the Crackup," I breathed to Chichak in the ambulance. "He took the suspect on all alone."

"Special Agent Diascu was taking you home when he happened to see the van driving away," Chichak said. "His radio failed. He engaged the subject, returned fire and was mortally wounded. In the highest Bureau tradition, he emptied his service issue at the subject. The subject crashed into the river. S.A. Diascu then effected a rescue of the victim. The subject died of gunshot wounds. You assisted him. and the Bureau is grateful."

I blew out a breath. Everything hurt.

"How grateful?" I asked.

The ambulance sped up.

The drugs in me started slipping me to sleep.

"Bess Van Leer will seek and obtain mental health care overseas," Chichak said.

"Mad Dog has a condo in Acapulco," I said. "Maybe they'll marry each other."

"The Van Leers will also go abroad to recover," he said. "It seems that you were correct. The subject did get Miss

Whippo's address from the victim. The victim says that he drove her somewhere, gagged her again, parked and left her. He came back running and drove her away fast. So he probably did see our FBI car outside Miss Whippo's home. When S.A. Fox challenged him, he ran.

"In the meantime, there's you," Chichak said.

He held up my wallet.

"Is this yours?"

I nodded. "I hope you didn't steal my Chirpin' Chicken Two-For-One Discount cards."

He slid the wallet into a pocket of my sodden jacket.

"It is possible that I can help you clear up your record and such."

"Do not fret my future, Wilbur. Where is the kidnapper right now?"

"Somewhere in the river. I saw his body float out of the van. The NYPD Harbor Unit will scoop him up for us."

"At Christmas time? Me, my flu and the holiday shopping season will be finished before you can arrange that. I wager that we never find him or his body. Maybe he will survive, get ashore and hunt the next family to hit."

"With bullets in him?" Chichak said. "I doubt it."

"And his accomplice?"

"Maybe he gets away. It happens sometimes. Real life is messy. But you are now in our good graces, and I can help you repair your life."

"That's the price of my silence, huh?"

"Silence about what?" Chichak asked. "I still have some influence with my people. We have unarmed jobs that require good detective minds. Have you ever considered working for the FBI?"

"As what?" I asked. "Your driver? For God's sake, Chichak, neither of us would survive that."

Special thanks once again to:

To Persia Walker, novelist, for her untiring help and suggestions.

To Detective-Investigators Mark Baldessare and Fareed "Fred" Ghussin and all the other cops and federal agents who taught me so much about hunting our real-life serial killers.

To the *Spy, the Movie* team – Jim MacPherson, Alex Klymko, Charles Messina and all the rest of the gang for a grand adventure in screenwriting.

To Irene Vanderwoort for her last-minute typographic rescue.

To Nad Wolinska for her as always inventive cover illustration and Richard Amari for his equally inventive cover design.

To my editor, Lynwood Shiva Sawyer, for his support and encouragement over the years

And my thanks to that wonderful woman, companion and friend from Guangzhou, China, who shares my adventures and my life.

The next Max Royster story is coming soon!

Bounced from the New York cops for mental disease and on crutches from rescuing a kidnapped debutante, I, Max Royster, cannot handle another Manhattan slush winter.

Freezing, grieving my lost shield, I hobble aboard an Amtrak train. America passes by outside my window.

When we reach the California desert, my spirits rise. Hope for a new life makes me exit in the small sandy town of Barstow.

The sun and beauty cheer me. But the town suffers from crime. A thug mugs me, taking my cash and ID.

That turns me sad again.

A group that I dub "My Showbizzers" – out-of-work dancers, actresses, dog trainers and writers – rescue me. They remind me of my live-for-the-moment cronies back in Manhattan, "The Playpen Irregulars." Thrilled by their energy, I fall in love with Koy, a beautiful Asian dog-handler.

Some Barstow deputies duck work or bully innocents. Their sloppiness angers and frustrates me, and their laziness helps a local criminal genius, Crostwaite, rob a bank.

Inspiration hits me.

My Showbizzers have many skills. Maybe they could use those talents and creativity to fight crime. They might do better than some lazy deputies.

Nobody else believes in my idea. Locals mock me. The sheriff and the FBI block me. But I force myself to push my idea forward, while my Showbizzers must fight their own bias against government and rules.

But when Crostwaite starts killing, I train my Showbizzers. They go undercover. Their beautiful bodies use sex as a weapon. Koy trains dogs to burgle homes and seize evidence.

To avenge his childhood of horrors, Crostwaite vows to destroy Barstow.

Frightened but passionate, without guns, power or respect, my Showbizzers and I risk everything to stop Crostwaite

Our deadly showdown will answer once and for all:
Can Showbizzers Crush Crime?

If you enjoyed *Brownstone Kidnap Crackup*, you might enjoy Frank Hickey's other Max Royster novels:.

Funny Bunny Hunts the Horn Bug

To catch a sex killer targeting Upper East Side beauties, misfit NYPD cop Max Royster goes undercover...as an NYPD cop!

The Upper East Side of Manhattan is one of the richest neighborhoods in the world.

But Max Royster, a maverick, outspoken and erudite NYPD foot cop, who grew up working-class in this tony area, calls it "the Playpen." Money protects the bluebloods in this area like the bars on an infant's playpen.

Late one night, patrolling wealthy brownstones, he sees a burglar attacking a rich actress. Max chases him. They fight but the burglar escapes.

The burglar is a sexual predator, known in cop-speak as a "Horn Bug."

For losing the suspect, Max's captain deems Max "a Funny Bunny," too unstable for police work. He strips Max of his gun and badge, then orders Max into Bellevue Hospital for observation and maybe for the rest of his life.

Without any tools or support, Max ten days to stop this Horn Bug.

The Gypsy Twist

"... Max looked carefully at the dead boy, reminding himself that most murder victims looked very young and surprised when their bodies were found, as if life had suddenly rushed up and taken them unawares ..."

Max Royster's hunt for a sadistic serial killer takes a startling turn when he realizes that not all predators are born alike.